NOW WHAT?

FRANZ WEINSCHENK

EVENING STREET PRESS
SACRAMENTO, CA

Evening Street Press

June, 2017
Sacramento, CA

Library of Congress Control Number: 2017934793

ISBN: 978-1-937347-42-0

© Copyright 2017 by Evening Street Press
2701 Corabel LN #27
Sacramento, CA 95821
www.eveningstreetpress.com

All rights revert to author upon publication.

Printed in the United States of America

10 9 8 7 6 5 4 3 2 1

Acknowledgements

Permission granted by Arizona State University to publish "Marimba Band."

Table of Contents

Accentuate the Positive, fiction	1
Homecoming, creative non-fiction	18
Just Another Day at the Office, fiction	34
Memories of Brooklyn, memorabilia	50
Norm, fiction	68
Madera, creative non-fiction	82
The Marimba Band, fiction	108
"If Music Be the Food of Love, Play On," memorabilia	119
Chris, fiction	128
Become a 'Late Bloomer' Like it Says in the Brochure, fiction	143

Accentuate the Positive

fiction

Normally colleges are accredited every four years, and that's what should have happened to us. But we screwed up so badly the last time they came, the accreditation committee only awarded us a humiliating two-year "probationary" accreditation.

Well, guess what? The two years are nearly up—which means that another accreditation team will be coming on campus, probably early this spring.

Our President, Dr. Cleveland Pinkerton, insists the whole mess two years ago wasn't really his fault. After all, when all this came down, he'd only been on the job for a year, which, he maintains, is hardly enough time to shape up a raunchy faculty. Furthermore, says he, the budget he was allotted at the time was just barely enough to keep the college from falling apart, hardly enough to make all the needed improvements. But then, our Board of Trustees doesn't want to hear any of that. They told him as far as they were concerned, it's the President's job—at a minimum—to see to it that the college of which he is the CEO comes through things like accreditations without any problems and to quit whining, complaining, and making excuses. Furthermore, they made it quite clear that as far as the up-coming accreditation was concerned, this time the college better pass—and with flying colors—or he too might "pass"—out of the picture. So there you be.

In the meantime, all of us administrators suspect that Pinkerton must be doing more than just a little bit of thinking about what to do when the committee comes round again—but so far we haven't heard much. One time in cabinet, he did tell us that he'd had a long talk about the situation with his minister, and then, some time later, a rumor went round that he was having an email correspondence about what to do with a professor from whom he'd had a class years ago.

Which brings us up to what happened just a couple of

weeks ago. He came to school one morning claiming to be a totally changed human being. What he told us is that he'd had an "Eureka-type" epiphany. It all happened to him very dramatically, he claimed, while he was driving home on the freeway the night before. While the sun was setting over the land-fill where our city dumps its garbage just west of town, everything, he declared, that had been so mysterious and murky was made quite clear to him. All that had been so complicated and puzzling was suddenly as plain as day.

The trouble with the college, he told us, was that from top to bottom and from side to side—the administration, faculty and students—all of everything was entirely too negative. "That's the whole thing in a nutshell," he said. That's the message he processed out there looking over our garbage dump. "As soon as I understood the concept," he told us, "I realized how true it is: Everything this college has done in the past—is doing right now—proposes to do in the future, is simply hell-bent on self-destruction. All we believe in is pessimism, skepticism and cynicism. All we do twenty-four hours of the day is to convince ourselves that the glass is half empty. Well, with an attitude like that, what do you expect?

"In this life," he continued, "as you must know, all the naysayers and toadies have programmed themselves to lose. Well, surely you understand that? How can you possibly achieve anything admirable, worthwhile, or noble if you define yourself as a loser. And you know what? That's the kind of mindset we had two years ago—and look where it got us? Well, I'm here to tell you that's not gonna happen again because I intend to do away with all the complainers, excuse-makers, and gloom-and-doomers at this college.

"Right now," he continued working himself up, "this college lacks the self-assurance and confidence to win. So from now on, I want only positive messages to get out there. Is that clear? Why not tell our students, our constituents, our parents, our taxpayers, and our Board of Trustees the good news for a change? Tell the world what's right with this college instead of forever dwelling on our short-comings and problems. Why not put our best foot forward? Why not accentuate the positive?"

Well, I hafta tell you, Dr. Pinkerton, "Pinky" to his friends, kept that up for weeks on end. By the time our first faculty meeting came around, he was just about in orbit. He practically bolted up to the podium like a wild animal and launched into his 'good news' peroration like the Evangel preaching to the heathens. "With the accreditation coming this year," he lectured, "I want us to be winners not whiners. I want us to hold our heads high because of all the good things we're accomplishing, not cower like beat dogs with our tails between our legs. 'Assume a virtue if you have it not.' That's what Will Shakespeare told us 400 years ago," he lectured, "and we know here was a guy who knew all about the power of positive thinking. Here was a guy who knew that today's good thoughts will translate into tomorrow's good deeds . . . What that means is that I want you deans and department heads to talk to your faculty, and I want you faculty people to talk to your students about the advantages of positive thinking . . . of being confident and constructive . . . of telling each other and the world about all the good things that you see going on around here and letting people know that we expect to pass this year's accreditation with flyin' colors—that we're gonna be winners not whiners, champs not chumps!"

And that's when he gave the signal to Barney Bailey, our audio visual technician, to flip on the overhead projector and flash the lyrics of an old Johnny Mercer classic up there on the big screen—and then motioned to Mrs. Johansen seated on stage behind a shop-worn upright, to launch into the introduction of the song whose words were up there on the screen. And the next thing we knew, he was jumping up and down like a pep girl leading us in singing the song which was to become his sacred anthem for months to come.

"You got to a-a-a-c-e-entuate the positive,
E-e-e-e-liminate the negative,
La-a-a-tch on to the affirmative,
And don't mess with mister in between."

*

He kept that up for weeks on end, but I gotta tell you, the truth is, well, I'm just getting a little tired of all this positive thinking around here. I mean, there are times in life when you're dealt some bum cards, and when that happens, it doesn't really help much to act like you got a winning hand because sooner or later somebody is gonna call you. Hey, but what do I know? I was just appointed a dean here a year ago, so the best thing for me to do is to keep my big mouth shut. The trouble is I keep having all these contrary thoughts. Like isn't the flip side of 'put your best foot forward,' 'hide the lame one?' Maybe we ought to rename Pinky's big crusade. Instead of calling it 'accentuate the positive,' maybe we ought to call it 'hide the village idiots!'—And speaking of idiots, believe me, well, we've got our share. The one that comes to mind immediately is Mr. Capps from the English department. Ron Capps is his full name. Most instructors call him "Madcapps." I can absolutely guarantee you that a guy like Ron Capps can easily scuttle just about anybody's accreditation. As a matter of fact, I've been trying to figure out what to do with him when they get here—maybe send him to a teachers' meeting some place in Lower Slabovia.

'Course, you'd never know it to look at him. He's tall, dark and handsome; speaks in low resonant tones like a TV or radio announcer, and always has great hair. I still shudder thinking about the first time I evaluated him. When you enter his classroom, you notice that he sits behind a small control panel by the side of his desk. Then, as soon as the class is seated, the lights in the room dim like in a movie theater, and some background music swells up. Soon, a large screen lowers itself smoothly and silently over the whole front blackboard and a video projector flashes the words "Reading And Writing Are Exciting" up on the screen. And that's when he passes out small glass crystals strung on beaded necklaces—one for each student. As the students start to put them on, he tells them in that sing-songy voice of his, "Feel the power as you put them on, people." And, as soon as the students have their crystals on, fifteen spelling words are projected up on the screen, and the students are directed to copy each word several times—not on a piece of paper with pen or pencil—but on the palm of one hand with the index finger of the other. I winced when I saw the word "rhythm" misspelled, but he still continued talking to them in that hypnotic monotone. "Remember, people," he droned on, "as we write these words on the palms of our hands, we can feel the letters enter our aura—never to be released . . . This thing is all-encompassing, people," he went on. "The words will forever be imbedded in your psychic computer. So remember that 'Feeling means learning to feel, and learning means feeling to learn.'"

As the period progressed, he flashed several paragraphs up on the screen and asked the students to copy them in their notebooks—a difficult task since the room was in semi-darkness. But somehow they struggled through it, and then were asked to exchange notebooks and mark each other's errors. "What is this?" I asked myself, "a lesson in rote copying?" Not exactly what I had in mind for a college class.

As the students filed out, I asked an older woman what she thought of her class. "Oh, I don't know what in the world is going on in there," she told me. "Everything is sorta' weird. I just do what he tells us and hope he knows what he's doin'. Not that he isn't a nice man."

*

Later, when the two of us met for his evaluation conference, I pointed out that I had numerous and serious misgivings about what I witnessed going on in his classroom. That mystified him. Quite to the contrary, he told me his lesson that day had gone smashingly well. "You know," he continued, "we've done in-depth studies on this thing, and it all proves out. In double blind studies, college students have improved by up to two grade levels on national norms."

"Well, Mr. Capps, I'm sure you'll get a few arguments about all that," I told him. "Especially from me . . . With all due respect, I think this business of rote copying in a college class is ridiculous. I know it's a remedial class, but I can't see anybody coming to a college just to sit around copying paragraphs. I mean, a person can do that at home. You could probably train a chimpanzee to do all that."

"Oh, this isn't all we do," he came back. "Later in the semester we'll actually be doing our own writing."

"Well, I'm relieved to hear that," I told him. "And did you know that one of the spelling words you had up there on that screen was misspelled?"

"Oh, that can't be true."

"Believe me, Mr. Capps, 'rhythm' doesn't have an 'e' in it . . . Look, you're supposed to be teaching these kids correct English, right? Not mistakes . . . These people make enough mistakes all on their own without you teaching 'em new ones. I mean, I was embarrassed for you—I was embarrassed for the college . . . And what's all this business with the crystals?"

"Oh, we all know that crystals help students improve much faster—up to two grade levels on national norms. As a matter of fact I use them in my own garden."

"You WHAT?"

"Oh, yes. We've found that if you place a crystal over a mound of vegetables, you get a much better crop. It's all been validated, Dean. We grow all kinds of perfectly wonderful vegetables—radishes, zucchinis, egg plants, squash, even award winning tomatoes."

"But you can't compare students with award winning tomatoes." I was totally exasperated. "Have you checked all this out with the head of the English department—about all these bizarre teaching methods of yours? . . . Look, I've been told that we have a definite and distinct course outline for the class you're teaching. And I don't think there is anything in there about rote copying, or stringing crystals around kids' necks, or award winning tomatoes! So please get this straight: From now on, I don't want anything happening in that classroom of yours that isn't exactly specified in that course outline. Is that understood?

"Well, that won't be hard to do," he answered, "because that's just what we do . . . You see, Dean, I was on the committee that wrote the course outline for that class many years ago—before you ever even set foot on this campus."

*

That's Madcapps for you—a ready but nutty answer for every question. And to prove his point about the crystals, for the rest of the semester, he sent a steady stream of vegetables over to my office—radishes, cucumbers, tomatoes.

I looked up his personnel file and found that every single one of his previous supervisors had checked "needs improvement." So I got a hold of Lillian Everly, our English department chair, who admitted that Capps has always resorted to unconventional methods. Though, when it came right down to it, she maintained, he generally taught at least the required minimum. "One thing is sure," she said laughing. "Madcaps rows the boat real hard . . . The trouble is sometimes the oars aren't in the water. This year, it's crystals. Last year, it was brain hemisphere dominance, or something like that—Half the kids in his classes were running around with cardboard patches over one eye."

Notwithstanding her mild assurances, I spent some time with Lee Snyder, our Director of Personnel, to see if there wasn't a chance to get rid of this guy—maybe assign him to work somewhere else in the college where he didn't have anything to do with students—like maybe in the library or the bookstore.

But all I got from Snyder was a frown. "You gotta understand," he grimaced, "it's damn near impossible to fire anyone for incompetence these days, especially in English. Remember all those English geniuses you got over there in that department go about their job in entirely different ways—some do grammar, some write compositions, some read books, some write research papers, some do creative writing, some do crossword puzzles, some write sonnets, some watch movies all day long. And that's only the half of it—which makes the standards and practices of teaching English a real nightmare, legally speaking you understand, quit untenable . . ."

"What I'm trying to tell you, Dean," he continued, "is that English teachers can do just about anything they damn well please as long as a lawyer can prove that just one of their hoaky students in any one given class improved even just a little bit . . . And on top of that, if you're tellin' me this guy's got tenure, well, you might as well forget it. Now if you could get him to fondle a coed or two up in the stacks, or maybe drop his pants in the cafeteria, we might have a case."

*

Time has a way of rushing by, and before we knew it, Christmas break had come and gone, and here we were already several weeks into the spring semester. And on a fine Tuesday afternoon in early February, right on schedule, the three members of the accreditation team signed into the Golden Pheasant Lodge, an upscale motel just north of town. Waiting for them at the desk were three weighty 350-page copies of our accreditation report—the result of Dr. Pinkerton's inspired campaign to put our best foot forward. Scores of instructors and administrators had spent days and days writing, editing, rewriting, and re-editing the thing. It contained everything anybody would ever want to know about a college—the mission statement, goals and objectives, organizational charts, job descriptions, duties and responsibilities statements, courses of study, flow charts, minutes of meetings, budget deliberations and formulations, student retention rates, activity calendars—all the minutia that go to make up a college.

Dr. Ralph Mueller, the committee chair, himself a college president, picked up his copy and thumbed through it. "This will make great bedtime reading," he said smiling as he handed his colleagues their copies. Of course we knew that Mueller was an old hand at this sort of thing. He does accreditations regularly. Several of our administrators had met him at a state convention. "He's one of the boys," they reported back. "Not going to be a problem." Pinky was relieved.

Next was Howard Hobson—the representative of a state-wide taxpayers' association—a business man, not connected with any school at all. Hobson had been journalism major in college and now owns a chain of computer and photography supply houses. We heard that he goes on at least three or four accreditations every year and considers himself the voice of the taxpayers. His reputation precedes him because he has this thing about going out of his way to find every scrap of printed material available at the colleges he visits—catalogs, course descriptions, student publications, brochures, schedules, instructions, bulletins, and minutes of meetings. If it's printed on paper, he'll find it—and lord help you if the t's aren't crossed or the i's dotted.

The third and last member of the committee was Dr. Lafcadia Weltgeist—a completely unknown psychology professor from a state university with no history whatsoever. All anyone could find out about her is that her colleagues considered her a bit peculiar. That worried Pinky. In an unguarded moment, he told us, "She's a shrink, probably full of psycho-babble like all the rest of them . . . You know, bubbling over with 'sublimation' and 'libido' and all that 'passive/aggressive' stuff—probably thinks the decline of student test scores is a direct result of improper toilet training— You know, most likely doesn't have a man around . . . God, as long as they had to pick a university professor to be on the team," he lamented, "why did it have to be a shrink? And a woman at that?"

*

The college went all out to make the welcoming dinner for the accreditors a classy affair. There were floral arrangements all around the gymnasium, real linen table cloths, beautiful china, hand lettered place-cards, glistening silverware. Each of us on the staff wore a large, shiny yellow happy-face badge with the words "Ask me!" printed in bold letters. A large banner stretched across the back of the stage right behind where the visitors would be sitting. It read "WELCOME ACCREDITORS." Each member of the accreditation team was escorted up to the head table by two college administrators. And to complete the picture, a harpist on loan from our local symphony, dressed in a stunning lavender gown, plucked away on her instrument.

"Is the harpist a faculty member or a student?" Hobson, who was sitting on my left, asked.

"No, I think she was hired," I told him.

He frowned and looked like he was about to say something but stopped short when he noticed Dr. Pinkerton at the mike. Pinkerton asked us to stand for the Pledge of Allegiance—then went into a number of lengthy introductions followed by two songs from the college choir. A tossed Caesar salad, chicken Kiev with scalloped potatoes and glazed carrots sprinkled with parsley, a soft bun, tea or coffee, and hefty pieces of chocolate cream pie for dessert.

At which point we all relaxed because we knew that the after-dinner program was bound to be a winner. It was a homemade video entitled "The Community College, YES!" produced by Barney Bailey, affectionately known around campus as "Mr. Media." Those of us who had seen it on previous occasions knew the visitors would be impressed with the panoramic views of the campus accompanied by an epic narration layered over symphonic music.

But unfortunately, somehow something went wrong with the video's synchronization that night because when the deep-toned announcer waxed eloquent about the view of the college's imposing skyline at sunset, all we saw was a group picture of the members of the Board of Governors—aging, paunchy, balding and mostly scowling. And then, when the announcer carried on about the well-endowed laboratory in the new science wing, what we actually saw was a close-up of some equally well-endowed cheerleaders at a football rally—a scene which elicited a splash of baritone laughter from around the hall.

Mr. Media was frantically pulling wires, turning dials and clicking switches at his control station, but his masterpiece never did recover before it came to a merciful but still out of synch conclusion.

*

Promptly at 8:30 the next morning, clearly identified with large, official-looking name tags, the three accreditors took off on their appointed rounds, but it wasn't long before the news of their activities circulated among the faculty. As soon as anything of consequence happened anywhere, it became the source of conversation in the teachers' lounge, the coffee shop, the mailroom, and everybody's computer and extension. Sadly, the news was not encouraging.

The first item concerned Dr. Mueller, the committee chair.

He was sitting in a class in Business Law when he heard an irritatingly loud and annoying grinding noise from out in the hall. Hmm . . . he thought. Very disruptive. And since he was a college president himself, he was hardly shy about investigating where such a disturbance might be coming from. Well, it turned out that the noise didn't originate in the hall but from an adjoining faculty office. And since the door was ajar, Mueller walked in and found Gil Davis, a psychology instructor, drilling through a stack of papers with an electric drill.

"What in the world are you doing?" Mueller asked.

Davis looked up, "Oh, just correcting some tests," he said thinking the visitor was giving him a compliment. "Yes, sir. Pretty nifty, huh?" he bragged. "You see, this is the way it works. I just put the template with the right answers on top of this whole pile of tests here, all 200 . . . like this," he demonstrated. "And then I drill right through the whole pile." Brrrrrrrrrrrr went the drill. "And that's all there is to it," he smiled as he lifted up the stack. "Really, neat, huh? . . . The number wrong are all those not on a drilled spot." He handed Mueller one of the papers.

"Neat indeed!" Mueller scoffed. "Why this is one of the wackiest deals I've ever heard of. Don't you people have a Scantron correcting machine?" Later Mueller got even more upset when he found out that Davis deducts the cost of that electric drill of his from his income tax claiming it's a necessary expense in performing his duties as a psychology instructor here at the college.

*

In the meantime, Hobson who was over at vocational education, had uncovered a more-than-questionable little kick-back scheme. It seems that the college was signing up students to become beauty operators and barbers and then sending them across town to a local beauty college which it had subcontracted to do the actual hands-on teaching. Officially, the students were registered here at our college, but realistically they hardly ever set foot on campus except for a P.E. class they had to take over at the gym. "I don't care if it is perfectly legal!" he bellowed. "From here on out, any student you guys register and get money for has got to be attending this school full time right here on this campus. Is that understood?"

Unfortunately, Dr. Weltgeist didn't fare much better. As she emerged from a sociology class, a boiling mad delegation of Native Americans greeted her out in the hall. They claimed that the anthropology department was digging up their ancestors' memorabilia in what they considered hallowed ground up in the foothills. "How would you like it if they dug up some of your grandparents' belongings and displayed them as 'artifacts' in some damned museum?" they protested. "It's bad enough when all these developers with their bulldozers tear up the foothills and put down strip malls and building pads and desecrate our ancestors' graves—but not a college? A college, like you guys, shouldn't be doing stuff like that! A college ought to know better," they insisted.

And that's the way it went for the whole day—problems, questions, protests.

But the straw that broke the camel's back came around mid-afternoon of their second day on campus. What got Hobson all steamed up was the memo he found in every faculty member's mailbox down in the mailroom. It originated from Campus Police Chief Petersen and read as follows:

From: Campus Police Chief Peterson to all college personnel:

I—"Relaxed Parking" For several years now we've had a relaxed parking problem during special events. Large events like athletic participation and theater crowds always request relaxed parking. That is why from now on parking will no longer be relaxed unless unusual circumstances can be demonstrated and shown.

II—"Moving Vehicles" the College Vehicular Code prohibits moving vehicles on walkways and lawns except if you are authorized. But even if a vehicle is not moving, it must be considered dangerous and hazardous because pedestrians could walk right into it as well as bicycles.

III—"Crime" This year your college police has been asked

more and more to open classroom doors by usually part-time teachers and instructors who forgot their keys. Please be aware that your college police has the priority job and mission and duty of fighting crime for innocent victims, NOT OPENING DOORS. In other words, "Crime trumps doors!"

IV—"Fire" Please don't call us when you hear the fire alarm. We don't know where the fire is either. Besides, when everybody calls us, it ties up our lines, so we can't call out to find out where the fire is."

*

After reading that, the three accreditors held an impromptu meeting in a corner of the faculty dining hall and started a rather heated discussion among themselves which was partially at least overheard by one of our cafeteria workers as she was mopping the floor near where they were seated. As a matter of fact, she overheard Hobson tell the others, "Boy, now I've seen everything! You know, at this point I can't really vote to pass."

"Maybe probation?" said the chairman.

"It all depends on English," said Dr. Weltgeist, the tall woman wearing the dark glasses. "And if English doesn't come through, this college is up to its armpits in doo doo."

*

The phone rings in my office. From its tone, I know there is some kind of emergency somewhere, some kind of crisis. I was right—Pinky was on the line.

"You are going to that English meeting, aren't you?" he gasped.

"Yes, of course."

"Look, we've learned that it's all up to English—the whole accreditation! Everything! One of our cafeteria workers told us. Your English meeting is absolutely crucial."

"Yes, I know. I know. It's all over school."

"Damn it," he said quietly. "I just can't believe this. How did all this happen? Why have things gone downhill so? Downhill," he moaned. I don't think I've ever heard him so melancholy, so low, so depressed—like he was going to break down and cry. "It all started with that video over there at dinner the other night," he said. "These people come here from all parts of the state, and all they're hearing are complaints and problems . . . All they're listening to are whiners and downers. Nobody is tellin' 'em one word about the other side. Not a single soul in this whole college is putting their best foot forward!"

*

All three of them sat up front behind a table facing a room full of English teachers hunkered down in the desk-chairs normally occupied by their students. They were very thorough: How do we test our incoming freshmen, and how do we place them into classes? How about remedial English? What kind of and how many classes do we offer? What are the goals and purposes of our curriculum? Do we teach grammar and composition and literature?—and reading and writing? How about the library? Do our students use the library? Do they learn how to do research? Do we encourage creative writing? And teach scansion in poetry? And do we ever follow up on our graduates once they get to the university to see if we prepared them properly?

For the better part of an hour and a half they drilled us on everything you might possibly want to know about our English program.

At the time, I thought we were doing pretty well. But then it's hard to judge how an operation is going when you're the one on the table. And then, all of a sudden, Dr. Weltgeist actually stood up, took off her dark glasses and told us that while she had read all our reports and listened to all our answers, what she came to understand is that yes, we were doing just about all that was expected—"just regular old white bread," she said. "You know," she went on, "the impression I get is that it's just 'business as usual' around here—the same old stuff we've heard so many times before and will probably hear again—All very ordinary—a bit hum-drum, don't you see—all quite predictable. Let's face it, the bottom line at this college is that nothing much new or innovative ever happens . . . Right? You have to admit it's all rather b-o-o-o-ring." She dragged the o-o-o's in that word for the longest time and made a face. "Where is the creativity? The risk taking?" she asked. "Aren't there any classes or programs like that?"

"That's exactly what I've been working on," interrupted Ron Capps who hadn't said a word all afternoon. The whole room turned to look at him. "I've been using some in-depth, three dimensional reading tests to examine our students and found that whenever we use solar illumination—students score much higher." He paused. "See here," he said, producing a set of three-sided cardboard graphs that joined together at the top like a pyramid. "This side represents speed; this side comprehension; this side retention . . . As you can see right here," he pointed, "by applying solar illumination, all three scores improve dramatically—as much as two grade levels on national norms."

I felt panic—a strange tingle on the skin—like the time a fish-tailing car came hurtling around a narrow mountain curve and just about sent us crashing over the edge. I looked at Lillian Everly, the English Chair, sitting right next to me, her face pale and drawn while her left hand continuously crushed a wad of tissues.

"Exactly what is solar illumination?" asked Dr. Weltgeist.

"Freeing the reading receptors in the frontal lobe by voltaic induction," Capps answered never missing a beat. "Here, let me demonstrate." And without the slightest hesitation, he took out a small green beanie from his briefcase. It had two small solar cells mounted on each side and a tiny propeller on top. After holding it up for everyone to see, he popped it on his head, fastened a strap around his chin, and to everyone's amazement, the little propeller on top started rotating.

"Ladies and gentlemen," he said, "the solar illuminator I am wearing right now is passing a small amperage over my reading receptors so that at this very moment I can read faster and comprehend better than I could just a few minutes ago."

I jumped to my feet. "Thank you! Thank you, Mr. Capps," I said. "Ladies and gentlemen, it's getting rather late, don't you think? . . . The committee must be exhausted," I told them. "We probably ought to be ending our session about now, don't you all agree?" I turned to Capps. "Ron, perhaps you can talk to Dr.

Weltgeist one on one after we break up."

"If she has the strength," Lillian muttered under her breath.

But, you know, that's exactly what he did. As folks were filing out, he walked up to the front of the room and started a conversation with the tall professor. And though it may be hard for you and me to believe, she was quite taken with him. And after some minutes, he took out another beanie from his briefcase, placed it on her head and fastened the strap around her chin. When I last saw them, the two of them were deeply engrossed in conversation, both propellers whirring in unison. For a minute I thought they might actually levitate—frontal lobe to frontal lobe.

*

We didn't hear from the accreditation team that night nor the next morning. They were busy writing their report. The schedule called for them to attend a light lunch on Friday at 12:15, after which, it was announced, they would run through their major findings but only briefly—no questions from the audience please—and then be driven directly over to the airport by one thirty.

Mueller started out by listing deficiencies, shortcomings, and concerns. Hobson continued with what seemed an endless catalog of sins. By the time the two of them got through, I figured we'd had it. Weltgeist was the last to speak.

"I agree with my colleagues," she started out, "that the college needs improvements, but you know, there is some distinct innovation going on over there in English," she said, "especially in the reading area. I just hope the rest of the college will consider doing some cross-fertilization with the reading department."

It was Mueller who wrapped things up by giving us the final verdict. "On the basis of Dr. Welgeist's report, and since English is the largest department in the institution, the team has decided to grant the accreditation—though, believe me, it was very, very close—two to one . . . In closing I must tell you, and this is very important—that all the problems you'll be reading about when our findings are published must be remediated immediately."

*

No sooner had they left for the airport, than Pinkerton

grabbed me by the shoulders and actually hugged me. Ecstatic, he shook me violently. "You did it! You did it!" he cried. "Your English people pulled us through. I knew you could do it! I knew you'd come through for the college!"

*

About a week later, I called Capps into my office.

"Ron, I've been hearing rumors that you're planning on asking your students to purchase some of these electronic beanies. Is there any truth to that?"

"Well, yes," he said, "we're thinking of recommending this thing. You know, it's all so awesome, Dean," he beamed, "really dynamite! What a tremendous breakthrough!"

"Mr. Capps," I said, "listen to me and listen good. Under no circumstances are you to ask any of your students to purchase electronic beanies or hats or wires or batteries or any other electronic paraphernalia. Is that clear? You're to forget about solar illumination, reading receptors and frontal lobes . . . Now that's a straight-forward, direct, unambiguous, and incontestable order, Mr. Capps—subject to severe disciplinary action. SO THAT FROM NOW ON, YOU'RE TO JUST TEACH THE DAMNED COURSE OUTLINE THAT YOU'VE BEEN GIVEN, MR. CAPPS! **TEACH IT JUST LIKE IT'S WRITTEN DOWN!** NOTHING MORE! NOTHING LESS! NOW IS THAT PERFECTLY CLEAR?"

"But I talked to Dr. Pinkerton just a couple of days ago," he said quite calmly. "And you know, Dean, he's quite impressed about this thing here. I mean, how can you overlook a gain of two grade levels on national norms? . . . And you know what? The other day he came over to our table at lunch and asked me where he could order some beanies—Now isn't that super? So I went ahead and put an order blank in his mailbox."

And then he reached into his briefcase, "By the way, Dean, before I forget it," he said, "I brought along some radishes for you and the missus. Nobody seems to be able to grow 'em this time of year—But then, you and I both know, when the crystals are on your side, you get award winning vegetables every time!"

*

Homecoming

creative non-fiction

It was in January of 1953 that I, then a Private First Class in the US Army, lugged my overstuffed duffel bag off the troopship "General Garwood," a converted tanker, down a gangplank and on to a broad dock at Bremerhaven. And that brought to mind a different gangplank—only we were going the other way—just about 17 years earlier—three German Jews—my hard-of-hearing mother Hedwig, my older brother Fritz, and me—climbing up a gangplank that got us on to the huge British Cunard White Star liner "Aquatania" with its four massive, tube-like smoke-stacks—Cherbourg to New York. We had boarded a train in Germany the day before, and as we were about to leave Germany near Luxembourg, two German uniformed inspectors stationed on the train searched us and our luggage thoroughly. They meticulously went through all of our exit papers. Thank God they couldn't find anything illegal or incomplete, so that they grudgingly approved us leaving Germany thus allowing us to continue our journey through France to the port of Cherbourg, where we got on that huge vessel which took six days to get us to New York.

Those were anxious days, and still today, we consider ourselves mighty lucky to be able to get out of Naziland when we did.

"Well, well," I mumbled to myself as I walked down that pier. "So now you're home again—back in the 'Vaterland'— 'Die Heimat'—back where you came from."

"I'll have to see Marie of course."
*

My base, though small, was beautifully situated in the Bavarian Alps. Only about 75 or so foreign language translators—mostly draftees—shepherded by a cadre of Army regulars. About a third were Mormons with language skills learned on missions; another third were German Jews like me who were lucky enough to get out in time, and the remainder a collection of just about everybody from everywhere. The Mormons came from places like Salt Lake and Provo, while the Jews, though recently from cities like New York, Boston, and Los Angeles, originally came from places like Frankfurt, Berlin, and Vienna.

But most unexpected of all was Paul, one of my three new roommates, Paul Popadopoulis, a. Greek translator from .Philadelphia, who had bright red hair and blotches of iridescent orange freckles that looked like they'd been splattered on his absolutely white skin with a paint brush. Who the hell ever heard of a Greek that looked like that? A native Greek speaker, Paul spoke English of course and perfect Spanish—and fluent Hebrew! It turned out here was the descendant of a bunch of Sephardic Jews who escaped to Greece during the Spanish Inquisition some five centuries ago, and whose family to this very day still keeps up both their Spanish and Hebrew traditions.

"So all this persecution stuff ain't nothin' new, is it Franz?" he laughed. This time around, his people had fled Greece just ahead of the Nazis.

My new home had been a German mountain artillery base, and I was surprised to learn that the Germans still used horses to lug artillery pieces through mountainous terrain during WW II. We converted their barns and stables into garages. With the Alps as backdrop, the scenery was spectacular, but freezing cold. A big stone eagle that had a large swastika emblazoned on it with its claws grasping a granite globe still lay half buried in frozen mud exactly where it fell when the Allies pulled it off the archway that served as the entrance to the base. The compound still used coal for heating and cooking which accounted for the sooty smoke belching from rows of hooded chimneys on top of all the buildings and the blackened berms of snow and ice that lined the company streets and walkways.

*

"Ja, Ja." said our cleaning lady—the "Putzfrau"—as she finished cleaning my work area. A portly woman with a stained kerchief covering her auburn hair, she wore a soiled work-smock tied at the waist with a broad brown leather belt—a bucket with a mop in it in one hand.

"Na, ja," she cajoled. "Such a good accent you have . . . Much better your language than the others. Maybe from Germany you are, ja? Von Deutschland bist du, nicht wahr? . . . Ah aber natürlich . . . of course," she smiled. "So tell us now, what place you are coming from?"

"Mainz," I confessed.

"Mainz . . . Ah, ja . . . Mainz of course, such a beautiful place! Then I was right, no?" she waggled her finger. "You don't learn an accent like you have in the school, huh? . . . Oh, but Mainz! Such an ancient and cultured city . . . Right on the river Rhine . . . Where they have all the river sports, no? Wonderful parks and museums . . ." She then took several steps toward me and spoke very confidentially, "But don't you miss it?" she almost whispered. "Don't you miss the authentic food? The Würstchen? The Rippchen? And the Kuchen?" she laughed. "You know, so wild are the Americans . . . Eat everything from the tin can, no? And so cold the drinks . . . brrrrr . . . Everything with the ice, no? No wonder they all are getting the ulcers."

At which point I raised my hand to stop her. "Now wait just a minute," I interrupted, "See here . . . Look . . . You have to understand. I don't miss any of that stuff you think is so great. Sorry, but being a Jew, I don't care for any . . ."

"What? You? You are a Jew?" She seemed genuinely surprised. "But you don't look it a bit!"

"Well, looks are deceiving," I told her. "So now just stop and think. If my parents hadn't had enough sense to run like hell when they did, I wouldn't even be here today. My whole family would have been murdered like all the others. Tod, verstehen Sie? Ganz Tod."

"Oh, ja," she put her hand up to her mouth as if in shock. "You are right. What they did with the Jews was so bad . . . so terrible! But then we never knew. They never told us . . . Bad politics, nicht wahr?" She started to leave, but turned at the door to face me one more time. "But then the Jews are lucky too sometimes, no?" she laughed. "Everybody knows it never rains on the Jewish holiday. Am I not right?"

*

And then there was the general. A real German general from WW II who had been one of Rommel's adjutants. We had supposedly "de-nazified" the guy so that now he could work for us as a civilian consultant. Shaved head, altogether militaristic, and very energetic. And so here I am, a lowly private first class with the power to call over a real general whenever I had difficulty translating some technical stuff, and he immediately clops over briskly and clicks his heels. "Jawohl!" he says. "At your service, Private."

And once a bunch of us GI's were sitting around on break smoking cigarettes and asked him how it was during the war—"Na, ja," he gesticulated, "German intelligence always knew, you understand. We always had the latest information—very precise, very current. We always knew what the French and the British were up to—ah, but of course. And we also knew what you Americans were going to do—without a doubt. Of course, we knew. BUT THEN, YOU NEVER DID IT! YOU NEVER DID WHAT YOU WERE TOLD TO DO! Some sergeant or corporal would tell you, 'Here, take this town.' . . . And you did it! . . . WITHOUT THE PROPER AUTHORIZATION!"

*

After a month or so, I got a weekend pass, bought all the coffee I could from the PX with my ration stamps and took off for Mainz to see Marie.

It's a long trip from Bavaria, but I was glad of it. Just to get some relief from all my new duties and routines—a chance to sit down quietly some place, think things through, and regain some balance. Though happy about having been assigned to Europe, I still couldn't believe they hadn't sent me to Korea. We all trained for Korea, not just in 'basic' but in 'advanced infantry' as well. Sixteen weeks of nothing but shooting, hiking, and bivouacking. Day and night—M-1's, carbines, machine guns, hand grenades, mortars, bazookas, anti-aircraft guns, wiggling through mud under live tracers, forced marches, night problems, bayonet charges, mock air attacks—not a day's let up. Boy, if I was ever ready, it was then. And at the end, when Captain Gallo had his meeting with our company and read my name to go to Germany, everybody gasped. Of course, I didn't mind. Heck, I was tickled. But while I was training in the infantry, I felt like a real soldier—hiding in fox holes out in the field, eating out of mess kits, digging trenches, sleeping in the open, trying to keep warm and dry, getting screamed at, running, jumping, up in the middle of the night to guard the perimeter, cleaning the mud out of my rifle—a real grunt! And now, of course, it all turned out different. Now it was more like working in an office.

*

The train kept pounding north. Though I had bought a couple of magazines, I didn't feel like reading. Just looked out the window musing, day-dreaming, wallowing in the luxury of doing nothing—just thinking about what the hell was going on. "Ding, ding, ding" went the wig-wag as we approached; it flashed by in a split second and immediately changed to—"dang, dang, dang" and disappeared. Intermittently it rained, snowed, and sleeted leaving the train cold and drafty. Glad I brought my Army coat.

Germany—they should call it Graymany. The country seemed transformed into monochromatic shades of gray. Always cloudy, hardly ever any sun. Leaden smoke over the roof tops in the foreground, layers of bleak dark clouds in the distance. It's as though an immense mass of gray pigment had been poured into all the other colors and possessed them. Gray cars, gray streets, gray people wearing gray clothing, shuffling through gray slag-stone rubble. Soon another gray train screamed by going the other way. You could smell the gray steam-smoke from its locomotive. "Ticket?" asked the conductor in his gray uniform. I pulled it out and looked at it. Guess what? It too was gray!

*

So how will it be to see Marie again after all these years? An orphan from infancy, bovine tuberculosis left her with a severe hunchback and a club foot. My folks took her in as a domestic when she was just a little girl to help Frau Memple, our housekeeper, take care of the house and Fritz and me. In turn she got a real home and became a part of our family. When she was sixteen, my folks sent her to seamstress school, and upon graduation bought her a new treadle Singer and helped her get started doing alterations right out of her own apartment in Mainz.

In 1934, a year after Adolf Hitler came to power, my father was able to leave for America on a visitor's visa, and that's when Marie volunteered to take the three of us in temporarily till we got our visas— my mother, Fritz, and me.

No doubt about it, in those days it took a lot of guts for a Christian like her to take in a bunch of Jews like us.

*

There was a boy sitting across from me in that train compartment staring at my uniform. I must have been just about his age back in Mainz when I got a taste of what the hell was really happening. In those days, all of us boys loved playing 'war' in the schoolyard. You draw a big circle in the dirt and divide it into slices like a pie. Each piece is a country. Then each player, in turn, throws his penknife down, and if it sticks in another guy's territory, he gets to annex everything from his territory up to the line where the knife was.

"I'm Germany," says one.

"I'm England."

"France."

"Sweden."

"Italy."

They crowd around the circle.

"You first, Wilhelm."

"Ja!" And he throws—'tzack!'—The knife pierces the soil vibrating with a whirr. "A hit!" he shouts. "Straight and deep— right through the heart of a Jew!"

"Christ killers," Arne adds routinely.

So Wilhelm quickly draws his line from where the knife hit and adds his gain.

"Again," says Arne. "You go again, Wilhelm."

"Ja!" He squints and throws—'tzack'—"Another hit," he

shouts. "Right through the heart of a Jew!"
"Christ killers," echoes Arne.
Mortified, I run away.
"Run, Jew boy, run!" they jeer.
But my friend, Carl, runs after me. "They don't really mean you, Franz," he says. "Only the rich American Jews."

But they did mean me, didn't they? Of course they did—and Fritz and my parents and all of our relatives—And the question remains. 'Did my guys really kill Christ?' They shouldn't have done that. What can I say? How can I make it right?

After Hitler came to power in 1933, things went down rapidly for German Jews. The country's commercial world was told not to do business with Jewish firms. Everywhere they fired Jewish employees and ostracized Jewish stores and professionals. So that after a half year or so, my father, who was in the wine trade, became convinced that he would soon lose all his customers and be forced out of commerce. Even though he was a wounded, decorated soldier in WW I, a respected local business man, and a classical musician, he was asked to leave the local symphony as well as several chamber music ensembles. The new rule was that in the Third Reich, Christians don't play music with Jews!

Soon, both Fritz and I came home with notes from school telling our parents that Jewish children were no longer allowed in public schools. So we attended a make-shift school in the basement of our synagogue taught by a couple of dismissed Jewish teachers.

And as you walked through the city, most stores put prominent signs in their windows "Jews Not Allowed," and often you saw editions of the notoriously anti-Semitic weekly "Der Stürmer," ("The Attacker," "The Stormer") mounted on prominent bulletin boards in plazas and parking areas. And on many street corners, there were large colored posters by "Fips," the notorious anti-Semitic cartoonist, of fat piggish-looking men wearing skull caps with big hook noses, grubby hands, and greedy eyes committing some kind of crime or abusing an innocent-looking young blond girl, with the caption "Juden Raus!" ("Jews Out!"). Meanwhile, we'd hear about elderly Jewish men being physically attacked by Nazi mobs—beaten up and made to shave their beards.

So that with things obviously getting worse day by day, my parents decided to leave Germany—he 55; she 45. I still remember them sitting around the kitchen table trying to figure out where to go—France? England? Palestine? Portugal? South America? They finally decided on America and applied for visas at the American Consulate in Stuttgart. And not too soon because—as we found out later—there were thousands ahead of us already.

It's hard to believe, but many of our relatives and Jewish friends didn't want to think about leaving. Somehow they talked themselves into believing that Adolf Hitler would not remain in power much longer. After all, he was such a wild man, so that surely the country would vote him out of office in the next election. Wrong! There never was another election. If anything, Hitler became more powerful, especially after the death of President Hindenburg.

And then one day, Father announced the good news that while he had to wait for his regular visa, he was able to obtain a "Visitor's Visa" to go to America. He would soon leave for New York, he said, to establish a 'beachhead' as he called it, and was convinced that all of our visas would come through in short order, so that we could follow him in a few weeks or at the most, in a month or two.

Soon, a heavy set man wearing pince-nez glasses, came to our house and glued little oval stickers with ridiculously low appraisal prices written on them on all our furniture, art work and silverware. The auction followed soon thereafter, and just about all of our valuables were sold for practically nothing.

A few days after that, Father left for New York. He was so sure that his family would follow soon, that he already went ahead and bought train and boat tickets for our journey to America. Meanwhile, the three of us moved in with Marie.

*

One day a few weeks later, Mother sent me to get some free mineral water from the fountain over in the park. By coincidence, it was a day that Chancellor Adolf Hitler was making a speech.

Every window and door was open. All the radios, at top volume, blared forth his grainy voice, his harsh message and the crowd's wild responses. "ONE LAND . . . ONE PEOPLE . . . ONE RACE . . . ONE NATION . . . ONE VICTORY!" he roared. And the crowd answered with wild approval. For the longest time they just screamed "Sieg Heil!" "Sieg Heil!" "Hail victory!" again and again and again in a frenzy of hypnotic adulation. Swastikas, flags, signs, banners, bunting, placards, uniforms everywhere in the narrow streets—blood red on steel black.

That night there would be a massive fire-brand parade on Hindenburg Street with troops, party followers, SA, SS, Hitler youths, military bands, even a brigade of the famous goose-stepping "Totenkopf" ("death head") tom-tom corps.

That's when Fritz told me he was going up on the roof of our apartment house and throw water on them, which terrified me! "Not that!" I begged. And pleaded with him not to do it.

"Such a stupid thing to do!" I told him, but he was adamant.

"You're sure to get caught up there," I told him. "And then what?"

*

"Water," I told Mother.

"Who's daughter?" she asked.

"Nobody's daughter," I screamed . . . "He's going to throw water . . . WATER! from the roof!"

Thank God she caught on and made him quit.

Time passed painfully slowly—month after month—and no visas. And now, it was almost a year since Father had left. The stress of it took its toll on her. Like so many hearing impaired people, she cranes her neck and stares at the speaker, makes out like she heard and understood, but never really catches on till later—if at all. Day after day she waits for that letter from the American consulate in Stuttgart—and day after day, nothing! And now the money from the auction is gone—and still no visas. So she gives Marie what's left of her jewelry.

But that Christmas, the two of them, Marie and Hedwig,

make a lovely holiday for the two of us. Here comes a small tree beautifully decorated with real tiny candles each in its own miniature candle holder. And Marie winds up her Victrola and plays her new record—the 'Toreador' song from the opera *Carmen*—over and over. I even remember our gifts—a tiny wind-up tugboat for Fritz and a water coloring set for me.

Right away we filled up the small sink in the bathroom and wound up the tug and watched it labor in the water. And got to rough-housing.

"Give it to me."

"No, me."

"No, me. I wanna do it!"

"No, you can't!"

And somehow it slipped out of somebody's hand and nicked the enamel inside the sink.

*

"What? What's on the blink?" Mother asked.

"No. Nothing's on the blink. It's the SINK—a chip . . ."

"What? . . . Something wrong with Fritz's little ship in the sink?"

"No, not a ship, a CHIP, a CHIP! . . . A CHIP IN THE SINK!"

When she finally found out what had happened, she was absolutely humiliated. Marie had taken us in, and now we've ruined her sink!

"Don't you understand?" she told us. "We don't have any money to give to Marie to fix the sink! Don't I have enough trouble with the Nazis? And my man gone thousands of miles away. And now you boys behaving like hoodlums and ruffians!" She started to sob and cry, and both of us were made to apologize to Marie. Sometimes I wished she would just smack us a good one and end it all. But no . . . she carried on like that for days and days.

*

And then one day, for no discernible reason Fritz was summoned to report at seven in the morning to a youth work brigade. He didn't come home by six that night, nor seven. As the time passed Mother became convinced that something had happened to him. Maybe they've taken him someplace? Maybe he's been arrested? Where could she go to find out about him? It all bewildered her, and before long she just broke down in a panic—started to cry and sob—and let it all hang out.

"My husband is gone! Our house, our furniture, the business, everything that was handed down to us, a lifetime of possessions, everything has been stolen and swallowed up by these thieves and murderers! They've taken it all—everything! And now my son is gone. Gone! Gone! Where is he? He should have been here hours and hours ago. Fritz! Fritz!"

Marie was trying to calm her when there was a loud knock on the door.

"You in there! Open this door immediately!"

When Marie heard that, she immediately hustled the two of us into the dressing closet she had there for her customers.

The pounding continued—so forceful I thought the door might break.

"Somebody in there talking against the Third Reich?—We'll just see about that!"

Marie pulled the curtain shut on us; then rushed over and opened the door. A brown-shirted SA trooper marched in. "I clearly heard someone in here complaining about the Third Reich," he shouted. "Would that party be you?"

"No," she said simply.

"That will not be tolerated! Maybe a bath in the Rhine is in order here . . . Who in the hell is in here with you?"

"No one," she said. "There is nobody here but me . . . See for yourself."

Mother was shaking. I could feel her body tremble. It made me furious. "Control yourself, woman, damn it!" I recalled what my father used to tell her whenever they argued. "Women, women—long on hair and short on sense!" I yanked on her dress and dug my fingernails into her thigh, and when she looked down at me, put my finger over my mouth, signaling her to be quiet.

He was still walking around the room. For a split second I

could see his spit-polished brown boots from under the curtain. If only Mother can hang on! At one point, he stood just a few feet away from where we were hiding in that closet.

"I could have sworn some she-swine of a whore was in here whining and complaining!" He strutted out into the kitchen, then in and out of the bedroom. "Ah, so . . . maybe from the next apartment." Now at the door, once again he traversed his gaze ever so slowly, surveying everything in the room . . . and left.

Fritz got in around ten-thirty.

*

At that very point, I could clearly see my mother's face in the window of the train as I sat there looking out. She now wears two hearing aids, each with its own thin wire that leads to an almost constantly squealing, rectangular black box pinned to the inside of her bodice. And has had two cataract operations, so that her large brown eyes are magnified several times over by the thick lenses of her new glasses.

"Mainz next," shouts the conductor.

*

When I walked up the street where Marie lives—where we used to live—I could see that her apartment building must have suffered a direct hit in one of its corners, probably where all the kitchens and bathrooms are located because all the way up to the fifth floor, there are sealed off gas, water and sewer pipes protruding in crazy patterns through boards and masonry. I found out later that on the ground floor, directly underneath Marie's apartment is a bar called "Gasthaus West" which caters to GI's and features American country-western music.

*

I couldn't believe how much she had aged. She was so tiny, so thin and drawn, her hair completely gray, her skin like a taut waxen film over pink flesh with delicate blue veins embedded in it. The deformity of her back and shoulders all came back to me, but I had forgotten that she limped badly and wore a high platform shoe on one foot. It was awkward, but we embraced for the longest time.

"My, my, how tall you've grown!" she went on and on. "But then Fritz told me all about you when he came by a couple of years ago... Just think, both of you boys in the American army! Who would have ever thought it?... So, Franz, they must feed you pretty good in the army... But then you always ate everything when you were a boy—not a fussy eater."

It wasn't long before the conversation turned to the war. "Franz, Franz," she said, "you can't imagine what it was like. Here in Mainz, during Kristallnacht in 1938, they destroyed every Jewish business in town, set Jewish homes on fire, arrested hundreds for no reason, and completely destroyed the synagogue where you and Fritz used to go to school. Then, a couple years later, they shipped all the remaining Jews to those horrible camps. If you folks would have stayed here, you and your mother would have been gassed—and Jacob Hugo and Fritz probably worked to death... They told the women they were going to get a shower, then cut off their hair, made them take off all their clothes, crammed them and their little ones into sealed off chambers and gassed them by the thousands! Not one Jewish person from Mainz has ever come back alive! Not a one!"

"And then, about halfway through the war, the air raids started... Franz, the air-raids were horrible! We had to go down into the cellar—sometimes for as long as four or five days—with no food or water or toilet—with people severely wounded, bleeding, in shock, constantly screaming, moaning, complaining—smelling of infection... And the dead bodies—ugh!—the stench of it is still in my nose. It will never leave me, Franz. You have no idea! And finally when the allies came, they would shoot you for a sniper if you looked out the window."

"And now I have to listen to that music from down there in the Gasthaus every night with those awful women... and noisy fights... military police... Ah, but we had it coming, didn't we, Franz? Even a baby could have told you this German madness was bound to end up in total disaster..."

"Must have been terrible."

"Ah, but enough of that," she said. "But you, Franz, you

were always easy." She came over and put her arm on my shoulder. "We'd give you a pencil or a crayon and some scraps of paper, and you would just go under a table or the sink and amuse yourself by the hour."

"The sink? You mean the sink with the nick in it? Is it still around?"

"Sure," she laughed. "Why not? We rescued it from out there." She pointed to where the bathroom used to be. "We put it in the old dressing closet."

"You mean the one where you hid us from that brown shirt? Where you saved our lives . . . and risked yours . . . Marie! Marie!" I got up and hugged her.

And then amazingly somehow I knew exactly where the closet was and pulled aside the curtain. Sure enough, there it was. Most of the enamel on the front of it was blown off, and it was awkwardly plumbed underneath what appeared to be the smallest water heater I've ever seen—maybe five gallons at the most. And I looked for the chip in the enamel on the inside of the basin. Not nearly as big as I remembered it all these years, but there it was. As I ran my fingers over it, I thought of Fritz and how the back half of his landing craft had received a direct hit on its way in to the beach at Normandy, and how everyone on board was ordered to plunge into the surf and swim to shore and face the Nazis without even a rifle.

"You remember when the two of us did this?"

"Franz, you were only children—little kids cooped up here day after day. Where else could you go? What else could you do? . . . It's nothing, nothing at all," she said. "Enough, enough now . . . Come, I have a little lunch for you."

*

That night we went through all the old photographs. I wanted to take her out, but she had dinner prepared—a dinner I know she had worked on for days. After dessert she brought out some sweet vermouth and a favorite of mine from when I was a kid—marzipan. And then wound up her old Victrola and played the record she had saved all these years, the "Toreador" song.

"Marie, you mean you played this record during the war?"

"Ja, but of course!"

I assumed a mock prosecutorial tone, "Madam, did you not know that in the Third Reich the Fuehrer has banned the opera Carmen? We don't glorify gypsy music here, madam."

"That got her to giggling. "Ah, Franz, Franz, you know what your father, Jacob Hugo, would say to that? . . . 'Kiss my . . .' (She formed the word with her mouth but didn't say it.) That's what he would tell you." And she began laughing and tittering and commenced conducting the record. And when the chorus came round, she sang along with the record as hard as she could. "Toreador-ahh . . . Don't spit on the floor-ahh . . . Use the cuspidor-ahh . . . What do you think it's for-ahh?" And that got her to howling with laughter even harder. But the exertion proved too much. Her face became flushed and she started coughing, panting and wheezing. Had to sit down and rest a while and collect herself.

And after a while, she looked up at me strangely and spoke very earnestly, "My God, the whole world would have been so much better if it hadn't been for Adolf Hitler . . . But then the Germans loved him, didn't they?"

*

I had a hard time sleeping on the couch. Boom, bam . . . Boom, bam . . . Boom, bam went the bass from the juke box downstairs—Joni James, Ernest Tubb, Margaret Whiting, Kay Starr, Roy Acuff.

The next morning, she let me take her to brunch before I had to take off. At the restaurant, she took out a little black felt jewelry case from her handbag and pressed it into my hand. It contained the jewelry my mother had given her.

"Please, Franz, take it and give it to Hedwig."

"What? Marie, please. I wouldn't dream of it. Never."

"No, no!" she insisted. "They're of no use to me any more. Believe me, there is so little time left. Franz, you have to understand; it's all over with me. I want Hedwig to have them. Otherwise, they'll only end up in some black marketeer's hands."

I opened the case: a brooch, two rings, a silver pin, a

necklace . . . little trinkets, rococo baubles, florid trifles . . . Probably too late for Hedwig as well I thought. Probably too damned late for all of us. And we embraced goodbye.

*

In short order I was back on the train going south, retracing my steps from yesterday. And somehow started wondering if they know—all the gray people out there. Had they ever heard of "the final solution"? About all those concentration camps? About the women and children whose hair was cut off before they took their shower in the gas chambers? About the brutal death of six million human beings? I figured if Marie knows, surely our "denazified" general down there on the base knows, as well as our chatterbox cleaning lady. And despite how they all try to avoid talking about it, they all know, don't they?

*

Somehow I was glad to get back to the base, back to my immediate boss Master Sergeant Alfred Knazovich, a highly decorated infantry platoon leader during WW II, who without fail goes on a raging two-day drunk every pay day . . . Back to our base commander, Colonel James Howell, a Bataan Death March survivor who spends most of his days reading comic books . . . and shaves his head in imitation of the Japanese major who was in charge of his compound. And back to my roommate, Paul Popadapoulis, who has bright red hair and bright orange freckles on milk white skin and speaks English and Greek and Spanish and Hebrew and always organizes poker games in our room after work, within earshot of the prayer meetings—hymns and all—from the Mormons down the hall.

*

Just another Day at the Office

<u>fiction</u>

    Yesterday was November 4, 1970, exactly six months after what happened at Kent State in Ohio last May. Remember Kent State?—where a bunch of shouting, chanting, demonstrating anti-Vietnam War students started throwing rocks at a National Guard unit? And the next thing we know is that the unit started firing at the protestors. Thirteen shot, four killed.
    And the reason we're reminded of all this is because of the huge six months' anniversary demonstration held just yesterday right here on our campus in the free speech area. Thousands of kids out there. Instructors telling us only about half of their students showed up in classes. The rest, out there protesting.

*

    Ah, but that was yesterday, and today is a new day, right? And despite the warning about an approaching storm our TV weather lady told us about this morning, I decide to take the bike.
    Now you know, I just got it in my head that at times like these that Schwinn out there in the garage really helps me stay half-way sane. I mean it's this damned war! Somehow it's taken over everything. Every night on television—in the paper—on the radio—everywhere, and forever on campus. What's going on in Vietnam is consuming our lives. All we're getting are demonstrations, protests, marches, teach-ins, sit-ins, and now the latest—bomb threats. Every morning some weirdo calls our switchboard and tells the operator there's a bomb set to go off in such-and-such a building on campus. At first, we got the fire department to come out to do the searching, but after a few days they told us they had better things to do, so that we administrators got to be the 'bomb squad' and every morning search and search for something we hope the hell we'll never find.
    So that's the reason I take the bike. Somehow I figure that with all this insanity everywhere, the 20 minutes it takes to get to

and from school on that bike will help me from going off the deep end.

*

Okay! So here I am pumpin' down First Avenue behind one of those smoke belching city buses, as I'm planning my day:

The absolute first thing has to be to finish the schedule of classes for next semester. Just gotta get that done—That's priority numero uno—has got to be accomplished TODAY—and no excuses! With our college so crowded these days, we have to justify the room assignments for our division so that all these other divisions don't get the idea they can just muscle in on our classrooms. I know they're just salivating to do so—can't wait to move us out and themselves in. "Well, look, they can just go screw," I say to myself out loud. "They're not getting any of our rooms! And that's final!—I mean, just because they have a lot of students . . . Hell, we've got a lot of students too!"

And then there are the faculty evaluations which are supposed to be on the President's desk signed and counter-signed by Monday—Not to forget the grant application for the piano lab. It needs to be completed before the first of the month—or we lose it!—Oh, yes, and of course, we have to be sure to go to the big English meeting this afternoon . . . I cannot believe it! These English people want yet another level of dumb and dumber English . . . Years ago we just used to teach 'bonehead' English for the kids who couldn't get into English 1A. But somehow, that wasn't enough—So we started a lower level bonehead class and called it 'Remedial English.' And now they want yet another class even dumber than that! What are they gonna call it? 'Fourth Grade English for College Students'? Good gravy, when is all this gonna stop? Why can't these high schools send us some kids who know how to read and write?

*

Right now I'm passing the big clock on top of the Chevrolet dealership on North Central—Ah, ten minutes to eight. I'm making pretty good time.

But then, all of a sudden, wow! The sky has turned really

dark, and the wind is blowing like crazy. Looks like a fierce storm is brewing. And before I can really think about it, 'plunk,' 'plunk,' 'clunk,' 'clunk.' Some hefty drops are bouncing off my helmet. And in no more than a couple of minutes, good heavens, it's pouring like somebody opened a fire hose up there. Man, is it ever coming down! That gal on television was so right. Taking the bike today was a HUGE mistake. So I hop off in a rush and fish out my old army poncho from inside my backpack, slip it on as fast as I can, jump back on again and start pumpin' hard. Before you know it, I'm sloshing through puddles being super careful not to let the end of the poncho on my right side get caught in the chain. If that were to happen, oh, man, what a disaster! And on top of that, by now my brakes are all wet and just about gone. Still, in about ten minutes, I make it onto the campus and ride across the free speech area where so many protested so bitterly just 24 hours ago. It's drenched and totally deserted. All you can see is the rickety platform on top of which so many raged so vehemently, so loud, and so long.

*

Well, when I finally slosh into the office a few minutes after eight, sopping wet of course, our division secretary, Mrs. Fernandez says, "Oh, my goodness." Never at a loss for what to do, she gets up and out from behind her desk and rushes into the storeroom to retrieve a towel. Good old Mrs. Fernandez. What would we do without her? But you know, this morning somehow she has a kind of serious look about her. Something is bugging her—I can tell. "Dean," she says in a low voice as she hands me the towel, "there's a very upset woman in your office."

*

That very upset woman turns out to be Miriam, a heavy set, middle-aged lady with straggly, white hair still wet and messed up from the storm. It turns out she lives less than a block from the college and claims that for the second time in as many months, somebody, undoubtedly a student, has parked their car in her driveway so that there is no way in hell she can get her own car out to go to work. "Dean," she bawls, almost in tears, "if'n somebody don't get that piece of crap off'n my driveway in the next ten minutes, I'll either smash all the windows out of it with a double edged ax I have sittin' in my garage, or spray-paint the son of a bitch with a can of international orange."

Wow!

Right away I call campus security, but they inform me that there is nothing they can do because the "scene of the crime" as they define what's happened, is off campus and therefore not under their jurisdiction. So I dial the city police and have Miriam talk to the dispatcher—luckily a woman.

That calms her a little—which is good—and after a short conversation, she hands me back the receiver. "The dispatcher told me they're gonna send an officer out to ticket the car," she tells me. "After that, I can call a tow company and have the damned thing hauled away," she says. "Only trouble is, right now the cops are so busy on account of this storm. Lots of accidents," she says.

"Look, Miriam," I tell her as I'm walking her out through the vestibule, "believe me, I'm really sorry all this happened. But you know what? Don't you have a friend you can call and maybe hitch a ride to work—or maybe take the bus—or call a taxi? Maybe you can call your boss and tell him why you can't make it today. Look, have him give me a call if he doesn't believe you. But Miriam, whatever you do—please—and this is for your own good—don't do anything foolish like trash that car! You got that? You understand what I'm trying to tell you? I mean, it'll just make things worse."

"I guess," she mumbles half-heartedly as she struggles to tie down the bandanna over her ruffled hair, once again prepared to rush out into the downpour.

As she's leaving, she just about bumps into Anna Marie Bengston, one of our English teachers, to whom something terrible must have happened because she looks absolutely awful. I've never seen her so upset. For one thing, she's totally drenched, her hair dripping and one of the sleeves of her raincoat just about torn off.

"The ceiling in my office caved in!" she hollers. "A bunch

of water must've collected up there on those ceiling tiles in my office—you know, right over my head—and melted whatever the hell they're made of—who knows?—cardboard or Styrofoam or whatever—and whoosh, a waterfall crashed right down on me! Like Niagara Falls! I mean I didn't expect it! Drenched in ice cold water! Oh, what a shock!—God, you gotta see my office, Dean—everything sopping wet—a couple a' sets of term papers I just corrected totally wasted, totally lost—compositions, quizzes, tests, homework, all my things and the furniture lost—the typewriter, my books, the rug—absolutely everything is gone—a complete, utter disaster. Good heavens, what am I gonna' do?"

So I ask Mrs. Fernandez to get her a cup of coffee and help her dry off, then hustle into my office and call maintenance. But the secretary out there tells me that her boss, the head custodian, is not on campus today.

"He's attending a sprinkler seminar in Bakersfield," she tells me.

"Man, he sure knows how to pick 'em," I grumble and I tell her about the waterfall out there in Anna Marie's office.

"Sure," she says, she understands, but there are several other emergencies on campus at this very moment. "I'll send Brady over as soon as he gets free," she tells me.

In the meantime, we settle Anna Marie in the workroom and Frances, who is our work-study student, and I hustle out through the downpour to Anna Marie's office—Oh, boy! She wasn't exaggerating. Her office looks like a tornado hit it. So we discard all the mushy pieces of ceiling tile, tie plastic garbage can liners over her typewriter, the telephone, all her books, piles of papers, and her little radio. Then put a big trashcan, lined with two plastic bags under the hole in the ceiling to catch the water which is still draining in. After about twenty minutes, I head back to the office and let Frances finish up.

I pour myself a cup of coffee; then go ahead and check the mail. Nothing earthshaking. A crusty note from Frederick St. Clair, the English chair, telling me that the big banner welcoming the visiting debate teams on the occasion of our forensics tournament last weekend had the word 'debaters' misspelled. "As you might recall, Dean," he writes, "there is no 'o' in it. When are these people going to learn to spell simple English words correctly?" he writes. "By the way, I hope you'll find time to attend our next English faculty meeting." Good old Frederick, he's fast becoming our number one curmudgeon around here. From what I hear he's really got it in for administrators; says they're simply an unpleasant reality instructors have to put up with. Says if they were totally eliminated, no one could tell the difference—Who knows? Maybe he's right.

"But enough of that," I tell myself. "You've got work to do! 'Member next semester's schedule?" But just as I'm walking over to get the folder with all the faculty schedules in it, BLUNK!—the lights go out! Not just in our office but everywhere—all over campus. Evidently, the storm has knocked out our electricity, so that all we can do is just sit here in our stupid office, stare at each other in the twilight, and listen to the rain pounding on the roof and windows.

"Damn," I tell everybody, "we might as well go home." At which moment, with the clock stopped at exactly 11:15, a thoroughly soaked student huffs in through the front door and shouts, "Dean! Dean! You gotta come quick! The electricity is off, and there's a couple of students trapped in the elevator in between floors over in Language Arts!"

*

So when I stand right next to the elevator on the ground floor and yell up to them, they can hear me. It's a girl and a boy. Thank goodness, they seem to be okay.

"We were on our way down from English," she yells, "when the elevator just quit."

"Are you sure you're okay?"

"Yeah," hollers the boy. "We're okay . . . We tried the phone . . . but there's no dial tone . . . the only thing that's working is the emergency light—probably got a battery in it."

"We're reading our assignment in English" she shouts, "Othello—you know, all about this super jealous guy."

I get their names and phone numbers . . . Tell them not to worry. We'll do everything we can to get them out of there as fast as we can. Tell them that as soon as the electricity comes back on, which will probably be any minute, the elevator will surely start working again.

Back in the office, I ask Mrs. Fernandez to call their folks and tell them what happened. Meanwhile I call maintenance again, and when I finally get through, tell the secretary about the stuck elevator. She replies that anything to do with the elevators on campus always goes straight to her boss.

"But he isn't here today," I interrupt. "Don't you remember? He's learning all about sprinklers."

"Well," she says hesitatingly, "I do have an emergency number for the elevator company. Maybe I ought to call them?"

"Yes, maybe you absolutely ought to," I insist.

"Okay," she says. "Get right back to you."

And to her credit, she does call me back right away like she promised. "The elevator people say they can't send anyone right now because their trouble shooter is on another emergency—but he'll come as soon as he gets free."

"That will not cut it," I tell her. "Can you give me the elevator people's number please. If they don't get out here right away, we'll just have to call the fire department." So she gives me the number and luckily I'm able to get the head elevator honcho on the line.

"Yeah," he snorts.

"Look, you gotta help me out here," I tell him. "I've got a couple of students trapped in one of your elevators. The thing is stuck in between floors in our Language Arts buildings."

"How many you got?"

"Two—a boy and a girl."

"A boy and a girl, huh?" He actually sounded amused. "From what I hear about those college kids of yours, they probably don't mind a bit bein' alone in that elevator, right? . . . You know what I'm sayin'?" he laughs. "Probably havin' the time of their lives . . . And now you want to interrupt all that?"

"Look, that's totally unacceptable!" I snap. "Come on now! I believe we have a contract with you people? And if you folks don't get out here immediately, I'm just gonna call our legal department—as well as the fire department. They'll probably come out here all right, and bill you." I was bluffing of course. Didn't know if we had a contract with them or not. And that's when he starts to tell me about all the other emergencies he has on his hands because of the storm, and how short-handed he is.

"Well now," I tell him. "I'm sorry about all that, but at this point I'm not interested in your problems. I want somebody over here immediately to get these students out of that elevator. I mean these are two human beings trapped in a tiny shoe box like that, and I want them out a' there—and right now!"

"All right! All right!" he answers grudgingly. "I'll do the best I can," and hangs up.

*

And just as I'm putting down the phone, through my office window I spy Brady, the guy from maintenance, heading our way. He's weaving his way through the downpour, coming to fix the leak in Anna Marie's office. With a ladder slung over his shoulder, he looks like one of those fishermen you see on the outside of sardine cans wearing a yellow raincoat, a yellow hurricane hat with the rim turned down, in black irrigators' boots. As he gets closer, I see he's holding a small coffee can with what looks like a tiny paint brush stuck in it. I suppose that's the can which contains the goop to repair that giant leak out there. "It'll never happen," I tell myself. "Never in a million years!"

So once again I slip into my drippy poncho and rush outside to intercept him.

"Where's the leak, boss?" he asks happily. "I'll just run up there and plug 'er up."

"Are you for real?" I ask. But even though this was probably a big waste of time, I walk him over to the front of Anna Marie's office. "Look," I tell him. "There's a major hole up there in that roof some place. You don't really think you can fix something like that with this tiny can of gunk, do you?"

"That's what they gimmee, boss. I just do it the way they tell me," he says setting up his ladder. "That's what they get for putting on a flat roof over all these offices out here," he says climbing up. "I told them when they built this mess out here to put a gable roof on it—Your flat roof will leak every time, boss," are the last words I heard before he disappeared up over the edge.

At which point I hurried back to the office, but just as I made the turn around the corner of the building, I'm totally startled to see a police car parked on the sidewalk right next to our front door. The motor is running, the red and blue lights on top are flickering away, and both windshield wipers are swooshing away fat raindrops, but there's nobody in the car.

It was on the inside, behind dark glasses and underneath a large white helmet, that I met Officer Patterson—at least so read his name tag. He had both Miriam and a student by the name of Becky in tow. Once he found out who I was, he recounted how when he drove up to Miriam's place to ticket an illegally parked car in her driveway, he caught her in the act of breaking into said vehicle—a blue 1962 Ford two-door—which, he explained, belongs to "this here student, Becky Edwards, who showed up just about at the same time."

"But I waited for you! Waited just about all day!" Miriam burst in, much agitated. "I waited and waited—for probably four hours—and when you didn't show up—and didn't show up, I got so frustrated I decided to see if there wasn't some way to get into that Ford so I could maybe roll it over to one side of my driveway and get my own car out of MY OWN DRIVEWAY—SO THAT AT LEAST I COULD GO TO WORK THIS AFTERNOON!"

And then Becky, who was young, blonde, and attractive, told her side of the story. "I'm sorry," she started out, "but I just couldn't find a parking space this morning. I mean, it was raining so hard! I just couldn't find anything! And I absolutely had to get to my eight o'clock biology class—Oh, you don't know! At exactly eight o'clock sharp my instructor doesn't just close the door, HE LOCKS IT! That means you cannot get a tardy in his class. No way! Never! If you come late, you're automatically absent! You automatically miss that class. And he allows you only three absences for the whole semester—any more and you're out! I mean, you're out of the class! Well, I've already used up my three absences, and he would have dropped me from class! And without my biology credits, I can't graduate . . . Can't get into dental assistant school . . . Look," she pleaded, her eyes brimming, "I'm sorry . . . I'm sorry for what I did . . . Really, I'm very, very sorry . . . I'll pay for the parking ticket. But that doesn't mean she has the right to break into my car."

At which point, Frances (You remember her; she's our work-study student) stuck her head into the office.

"Dean, Dean," she hollered, "The elevator man is here lookin' for you."

*

So I excuse myself, duck into the outer office over to Mrs. Fernandez's desk. "Mrs. Fernandez, would you see what you can work out with the folks in there? Look, I've got to get those kids out of that elevator . . . Be back as soon as I can."

Once again I'm out in the rain, although by now maybe it's let up a little. I jog around the squad car with its motor, wipers, and crazy lights still doing their things, and jump into the elevator man's pickup.

*

He has a distinct Irish accent. "Whare is it now?" he asks, "the elevatorr whare the young people are holed up?"

"Right over there in Language Arts," I tell him pointing the way through some pretty large puddles.

And just as we're walking down the dark corridor on the ground floor of Language Arts on our way to the elevator, with an audible 'click,' lo and behold, the electricity snaps back on.

"Hey!" I holler. "Hallelujah!" I shout. "You did it! You fixed the electricity!" I tell the Irish guy. "All right! Now we can get 'em out! Right?"

Wrong!

He pushes and pulls every button, handle and switch on the outside of the elevator and shouts up to them to do the same on the inside—BUT NOTHING! ABSOLUTELY NOTHING! He thinks the motor is shot—probably shorted out by some water from somewhere.

"Well now," he says, his blue eyes twinkling, "with the motorr out, ye understand, there's no other way to get that elevatorr down from thare, than by sheer force of grravetee." And goes on to explain that there is a brake which if released, will let the elevator down. But you have to baby it down very slowly—gently—little by little; otherwise it will crash down to the basement. And there are two other problems he continues. One is that when you lower the thing, you have to stop exactly at the point where the inside door matches the outside landing; otherwise you can't get the outside door open without breaking it down. And on top of that, and most problematic, the braking mechanism is way out in back of the building so that the person working it really has no way of knowing exactly when to stop lowering. "Now we've got a little leeway, ye underrstand," he gesticulates, "maybe six orr eight inches. But if ye miss it by too much, ye have to send the bloody thing clearr down to the basement, break down the door on top and rescue yer stranded people through the rroof of the elevatorr."

Oh brother! I look at my wristwatch. It's already after one which means that those kids have been in that stupid thing for well over two hours.

At which point Frances comes over with a message from Mrs. Fernandez.

"Dean," she says, "Mrs. Fernandez told me to tell you not to forget about the English meeting. It'll be starting in just a few minutes."

"The English meeting! Are you kidding? The English meeting! Who in the hell can go to an English meeting at a time like this? Hell, for once they'll just have to get along without me. Do 'em good . . . Frances, how are things in the office?"

"Oh, Mrs. Fernandez has everything all fixed. Everybody's dropping all charges."

"They are? . . . Wonderful! How in hell did she manage

that? I'm telling you that woman is a saint . . . Frances, look, don't go anywhere. I'm gonna need you."

By this time the Irish guy has everything all figured out—that is how to get the kids out. He tells us that we will have to organize ourselves into a human chain from the front of the elevator all the way to the back of the building where he'll do the lowering. And when the inside elevator door is just about even with the outside ledge, the kids on the inside will have to yell "Now!" which is the signal to start the chain—that is everybody hollering loud and fast to the person down the hall from them and around the corner to where he'll be ready to slam on the brake.

So Frances and I start recruiting any and everybody we can find to be in the chain while he explains everything very clearly to the kids inside the elevator. We grab Anna Marie and Mrs. Fernandez and Miriam and Becky from the office. Frances even tries to recruit Officer Patterson, but he's in his squad car writing up his report with the motor running.

Ah, and here comes Brady just down from the roof with that ladder over his shoulder still looking like a drowned fisherman. He tells us he doesn't think he's got enough goop to stop the leak over Anna Marie's office. "No kidding," I tell him. "Well, never mind that now. You'll fix it tomorrow. Right now, look, we need you in the chain," I tell him and hand him over to Frances who has him put down his ladder and walks him into the chain down the hall.

So that in just a few minutes, we're all set. "Everybody ready?" I holler, and hear a bunch of "Yes's" and "Okay's." And that's when the Irish guy starts lowering the elevator—very slowly, little by little.

Suddenly I can hear the kids shout from inside the elevator "We're almost there," they holler. "Only about eight inches more . . . six . . . four . . . NOW! NOW! STOP! STOP IT!"

"NOW!" repeats Frances to Anna Marie.

"NOW!" echoes Anna Marie to Mrs. Fernandez.

"NOW!" Mrs. Fernandez yells to Miriam.

"NOW!" Miriam passes on to Brady.

"NOW?—NOW WHAT?" Brady looks puzzled.

"NOW STOP THE DAMNED THING!" I scream for all I'm worth. Luckily the Irish guy out back hears me and slams on the brake.

"No need to get mad," Brady grumbles. "You know this would'a never happened if'n they had just bought a decent elevator in the first place."

But nobody was paying attention to Brady 'cause we're all running over to the elevator door. Luckily it didn't pass the ledge by too much and our Irish friend is able to open the door. Hooray! Look, there they are. All they have to do is step up a couple of inches and THEY'RE OUTA THERE!

"Yeah," the young guy says, and everybody cheers and applauds.

They turn out to be pretty average college kids—not trendy or nurdy or zany like everybody expects.

"Man, you guys have been in there a long time," I tell them, "and don't even look a bit frazzled or upset. Like it's something you do every day."

"Oh, we knew everything was gonna be all right," the girl says modestly, "and, you know, we even got our homework done."

"Homework?" jibes Frances, "Oh, come on now. You mean you two—a grown man and a mature woman—all by yourselves in that tiny little space all day—and you're tellin' me you did homework? You mean you didn't even fool around a little bit? Come on now—not even a tiny little bit?" Everybody laughs.

"And besides, didn't you have to go to the bathroom?" asks Becky. More laughter.

"So, are you gonna sue the college?" Miriam chimes in.

"I think you should," Frances agrees. "You know, you've got a dynamite case. I mean, locked up in solitary confinement for all that time. "God knows, you could've gone bonkers in there."

*

So I invite them over to the office, and while Mrs. Fernandez brews us all some fresh coffee, I have each of them call their parents again—but still no luck. And after we finish our coffee, I walk them out the door. Hey, what do you know? The weather is starting to clear up.

*

Once back inside, I ask Mrs. Fernandez, "Tell me now, how in the hell did you do it? You know, that whole mess with Miriam and Becky and Officer Patterson?"

"Well, I figured since they both broke the law, if neither one pressed charges, the officer was simply out of business."

"A genius! That's what you are! The two offenses canceled each other out, right?—Beautiful—Maybe life works out that way sometimes . . . Say, what time is it anyway?" I look up at the clock. "What! Four-thirty! I can't believe it—seems like I just got here."

"Maybe you feel like you just got here," she says, "but I feel like I've been here all my life!"

*

At which point the phone rings. It's the head custodian back from the sprinkler wars. I catch him up on everything—the leak in the roof—the whole mess with Miriam and Becky and Officer Patterson—the stuck elevator—the whole nine yards. And that's when he starts to tell me about his day. Well, you can't just hang up on somebody like that, but, you know, a long time ago I learned how to talk on the phone by just making small talk, you understand, saying stuff like "yeah, yeah, yeah," and "sure, sure, sure," while concentrating on something else. This time I'm browsing through all my phone messages for the day. Mrs. Fernandez puts them on a spindle. Three are from my immediate boss, the Dean of Instruction, and one is from the President. Hmmm—wonder what he wants?

And just as I'm getting off the phone, I spy a note addressed to me on the edge of my desk. It's from my old buddy Frederick St. Clair, the English Chair.

"Dear Dean, It's extremely unfortunate and regrettable that even at this critical juncture in our department's deliberations about a new level of remedial English, the Dean of the Division chooses to absent himself from our colloquy. Whether by design or through carelessness, your absence from our discussion cannot but be interpreted in any other fashion than another crass example of your consistent and cavalier disdain for the importance of the work of our department. 'Nero fiddles, while Rome burns!' Sincerely, Dr. Frederick St. Clair, English Department Chairperson."

I get out my fat marking pen. "Wrong!" I scribble on the note. "The English chair babbles, while the college drowns! Send me the minutes. Love. Your friendly Dean." I dash his name on, and toss in the out-basket.

*

And then for some reason, my little side table catches my attention. It's been waiting patiently all day with an almost toppling stack of manila folders piled one on top of another—next semester's schedule, the evaluations, the piano lab. Not one iota of work has been done to advance any of these—not a single item—absolutely nothing! There they lie, those fat little manila folders, peering at me ominously, just like they did last night. The storm has taken a day out of our lives. And while we were desperately bailing out our little dinghy, I'm sure others were making headway, consolidating their positions—and figuring out how to get their grubby little hands on our classrooms.

"Enough of this crap!" I holler. "Let's lock her up, Mrs. Fernandez. 'The evil of the day is sufficient thereunto!' Maybe we'll get lucky tomorrow and have an earthquake or an insurrection or whatever!" For a brief moment the thought of taking home a folder or two crosses my mind. "Ah, screw it!" I mumble. "They don't pay you enough!"

*

By the time I get to my bike, the rain has stopped, and a brisk north breeze is dispersing the clouds. I climb on the seat which I had covered earlier with a plastic garbage can liner and head back out over the free-speech area on my way home. Two quotes come to mind. One: "Some days it don't pay to get out of bed." Two: "To err is human, but to screw up royally takes team work!"

*

As I pump into that stiff but delicious headwind, I imagine

that each breath of this clean, fresh, after-the-rain air is helping to expunge irritation, frustration, and self-doubt. And I say to myself, "In comes the good air; out goes the bad. In comes patience, good cheer, and decency—Out goes hubris, pettiness, and Frederick St. Clair, the English chair.

And then I notice a large crumpled placard still left over from yesterday's demonstration stuck half-way down a sewer drain. All I can see are two words: VIETNAM—OUT! And it reminds me that Jeff will be 17 next January, only a year away from the draft. If he can get into college, he can get a deferment, but he's flunking French and always in trouble with coach out there in PE because he and his buddy Kenny don't want to pick up the trash and empty beer cans at the stadium after the football games. "That's not the students' job," he tells me. And even if he does get into college, I wonder if he would join those kids who taunted the National Guard that day last May—defied and cursed and threw rocks at them—then heard the almost silly little pop, pop, pop's of their rifles and buckled to the ground, probably not even aware of the smell of sulfur smoke from the discharges . . . or their friends' cries of surprise, disbelief, and horror.

*

Memories of Brooklyn

memorabilia

It's May, 1935, and here we are three German Jews—our mother Hedwig, my older brother Fritz, and me—just crossed the Atlantic on the huge, four smoke-stacked Cunard White Star liner SS Aquitania, Cherbourg to New York. She's 47, Fritz 14, and me—I'm nine. Not that many years later, both Fritz and I would be returning back to Germany, but this time in US Army uniforms, he on D-day on Normandy Beach and me during the Korean War.

It took at least a half-dozen powerful tugs to dock that mammoth ocean liner, but once they did, the passengers started filing down the gang plank on to the pier. But not us. We're still on board, up on the main deck waiting for Mother who is being examined by the US Immigration Service inside a lounge right next to where we're standing. From our vantage point, we can see the unbelievable skyline of New York—Wow! What a place!

Still it seems like Mother has been in there forever—more than an hour, and we're getting anxious. She's very hard of hearing, can't speak a word of English, and that worries us. I'm thinking maybe she's going to fail her physical—or can't hear or understand what they're telling her—or they can't understand what she's telling them—or something else is wrong. Maybe our papers are screwed up—or the quota is filled—or whatever—and we'll all get sent back to Naziland. God!

After about another half-hour, we see our father, Jacob Hugo, all five feet one inch of him, coming up on board. He's been living in New York for almost a year. Came over on a visitor's visa. Hope he's got a regular one by now. Ah, but it's great to see him. We hug.

"Where is your mother?" he asks nervously, and we tell him she's inside being examined by the immigration people.

"She's been in there forever," I tell him.

"So why isn't she coming out?" he mumbles and walks into the lounge to talk to somebody. I try not to say anything, but being a worry-wart, I agonize about what will happen if they turn her down. And why is it taking so long? In the meantime, all we can do is wait; so that's what we do –wait and wait, and wait some more.

Somehow there is this German couple, probably tourists, standing near us also looking at the New York skyline. Both of them are wearing long black leather coats and wide-brimmed leather hats. The man sidles over. "So," he asks in German, "German boys you are, nicht wahr?"

"Ja," Fritz answers.

"So then, what are your names?"

"Fritz," he tells him.

"And you?" He looks at me.

"Franz," I tell him.

"Fritz and Franz!" he laughs. "Ah, such authentic German boys. So when to the Vaterland will you be returning?" he asks.

"No, we're waiting for our mother," Fritz tells him. "Going to be living in New York."

"Oh, no! Nein, nein," he says. "You need to tell Mutti to take you back home," he says. "That is where real German boys like you two—Fritz and Franz—belong. Nicht wahr? Am I not right?"

We don't say anything, just walk away and over to the other side of the ship; then back around and into the lounge. And what do you know? Just as we do, here she comes—out of the door behind where the immigration people have set up their desk. And when she sees us she smiles broadly! To me that means she passed, right? YES! YES! SHE MADE IT! Mother and Father embrace. She passed! Everything is okay. She made it! We made it! They won't send us back! Thank God!

By the time we walk down the gang-plank onto the pier to collect our luggage, most everybody has left—But we're elated because we're going to be living in New York City! Yes! We're here! We finally got out of that hell hole over there and made it to America! God bless the United States of America!

*

Our first meal is in an automat. You get to choose from an

assortment of dishes inside little glass cubicles. Coins clink, you open little glass doors and carry your food to your table and eat it. Then there is the long ride on the subway. We get on the Sea Beach Express to Brooklyn guarding our luggage like mother hens and get off at the 59th Street station on Fourth Avenue; then haul everything over to where we're going to be living on the second floor of a house on 61st Street between 5th and 6th Avenues. The place has steam heat, an ice box, a stove with an oven, and an out-of-use dumbwaiter.

But the main thing is that we survived. We made it! We're alive. About 3,000 of the 4,500 Jewish people who lived in and around our hometown, Mainz, with its approximately 350,000 inhabitants, would not make it. In the next six years they would be sought out, humiliated, disgraced, persecuted, physically attacked, their property confiscated, and finally put into box cars and sent to concentration camps where they were either brutally worked, starved, beaten, shot, or gassed to death. None of them ever returned to Mainz. Their only crime? being born Jewish. Sometimes it makes me feel guilty that I and my family made it—that we are now lucky enough to live in a place where people don't just automatically hate your guts and want to kill you.

*

My folks get the one bedroom, and Fritz and me sleep on the couch in the living room which makes up into a double bed.

And it's great to see Father again. We catch him up about our year-long wait for our visas from the American consulate in Stuttgart, and he tells us about his struggles to get work, about the deep depression America is in, and how, although he's made a tiny bit of money here and there selling American wines from California overseas, he's basically failed to make a living.

I can see he's upset. He's aged. His eyes look strained—his voice anxious. He's worried about not having a regular job, not bringing home a paycheck. He knows his English isn't all that great. Sure, he tries to act confident and positive, but the hard fact is that the only money coming in is from commissions on sales—and there are hardly any of those. How can you blame him—a man in his mid-fifties who knows he's failing at being the family's provider but still tries so hard and worries so much?

The next morning, Fritz and I go out to take a look around the neighborhood. When the kids on our block see us, they start laughing, jeering and hooting. It's Fritz's short pants. In Germany all teenagers wear pants like that, but here in Brooklyn, shorts are only for little kids like me. It's not a good beginning. We retreat back home so he can change into the only pair of long pants he owns. The encounter sets a sour tone with him. From that time on, he mainly develops friends that are older, often from the high school he goes to—Manual Training High—not the kids on the block—Ah, but not me!

For some reason Jackie McPortland, a kid about my age who lives on the ground floor of our building wants to be my friend, and even though I know no English, he helps me get in thick with the boys on our block. I start wearing a baseball cap just like they do. My parents can hardly get me to take the thing off even at the dinner table. It's a symbol of my new identity—a Brooklyn Dodger fan. I even go to bed wearing the dumb thing. I learn how to play stickball, though badly, and handball at which I'm a little better. We play against the wall of a big apartment house that has a large sign on it "Positively No Ball Playing," but nobody pays any attention.

For the first couple of weeks, Father becomes our tour guide. He walks us around the streets of Manhattan, and they really do take your breath away—skyscraper after skyscraper—concrete, steel and glass. We peer through the telescope atop the Empire State Building—360 degrees of unbelievable buildings with avenues like canyons in between them—extended bodies of water in the distance. At a juice bar in Times Square, he buys us each an orange juice that's freshly squeezed right there in front of us. In Germany, you never see an orange except maybe at Christmas. The streets are so crowded, for a time I become separated from them and panic. How will I ever be able to find my way back home? Luckily we re-connect. We ride the ferry over to Staten Island right in front of the Statue of Liberty with Manhattan's skyline in the background. On the weekend we go swimming at Coney Island, and Fritz gets nabbed by a woman cop for changing into his swim trunks under the boardwalk. She chews on my folks for a while.

Next he takes us to the aquarium in Battery Park where the bums hang out; wants to show us the electric eel. It's a long slimy green thing in a big tank that peers out at you from under a rock. There's supposed to be a demonstration every hour. When the attendant finally arrives, he repeatedly pokes a stick at the thing till it gets mad enough to emit a little electricity into the water, just enough to light up a tiny bulb on the side of the tank. "How about that?" Father beams. "Really something, Nicht wahr?" America has come through!

The long block where we live in Brooklyn, 61st Street between 5th and 6th Avenues, has several series of two-story homes built right next to each other—each house being exactly the same as its neighbor—brownstone staircases that lead up to the first floor landing—like townhouses. To get to the second floor where we live, you have to go up the outside staircase, enter through the first story front door and walk up another flight on the inside. The front room on each floor has a bay window that looks out on to 61st Street. All the houses are dark brown with light brown sash and trim and the same black curlicue wrought iron banisters on the outside staircases, the same gray metal garbage cans set in exactly the same spot on the street level concrete porches they call "aeries."

When school starts that fall, we realize how Irish our neighborhood is since Fritz and I are just about the only kids on the block who go to public school. The other kids all go to the big K-12 Catholic school complex located right next to one of the largest churches ever—"Our Lady of Immaculate Conception."

Had I stayed in Germany, I would have been in the 5th grade, but since I don't know the language, they ship me back to the second grade, and for the next three years, every few months or so—as my teachers think I'm catching on—they move me up a half grade—from 2A to 2B, from 2B to 3A and so on. Each time I have to leave the few new friends I made in the previous class and start over again with a new teacher, new students, and a new system.

I don't remember a day that I don't have to go to the bathroom sometime during the morning or afternoon but too embarrassed to ask. It's tough holding it, and sometimes I don't make it. And once on my way home from school, I see this sign on an apartment house which says, "Room To Let." I thought that meant they had a room with a toilet and went up and asked.

"Heavens no, child!" she said and slammed the door.

*

We rent from the McPortlands: $36.00 a month. Three generations of McPortlands occupy the bottom two floors. And one afternoon, when I come home from school, there is a large funeral wreath hanging from the door on top of the outside steps—Grandfather McPortland has died. When I open the door, there he is. They have opened the two sliding doors from their first-floor front room to the hallway, and I cannot pass without being in his presence. I had never seen a dead man like that. He looks so real and lifelike—like he might get up any minute and say hi to me like he did just a few days ago. And what shocks me most is that there are all these people sitting around eating and drinking and laughing and talking so loud. I thought you were supposed to be solemn and quiet in the presence of death.

*

The subways of New York are always crowded and noisy. For a nickel you can ride all day and never go over the same tracks twice. Even at two or three in the morning, the cars are filled with people of every size, color and description—coming and going. Like the arteries of a raging beast, the New York subways pump humanity like cells from its core to its extremities and back again nourishing the city's insatiable appetite. People always seem to be on urgent business. They hurry, they run, sometime even sprint to make connections. Even before their train arrives, they huddle in tight knots at the track's edge knowing that one of the doors of their particular train will open exactly where they're standing. Their train rushes into the station with a great swoosh but brakes precisely on its appointed spot. Instantly the doors roll open; some people wiggle out; others charge in. Often the cars are so full there doesn't seem room for even one more person. So those left outside turn their backs on the mass of humanity inside and push backwards as hard as they can and somehow force their entrance. By the time the doors struggle to close, the crush is paralyzing.

As I'm standing there in about the middle of a car, pinned in tight from all sides, I feel a hand on my buttocks, invading and exploring. Terrified, I bolt and fight my way past annoyed passengers to the other end of the car and glance back, but it's impossible to tell; they all look equally indifferent. Those lucky enough to get seats close their eyes or read. The rest of us hang on to posts or leather straps hooked on to overhead rails like dangling carcasses. Some read newspapers folded into narrow columns so as not to take up too much room. Their neighbors steal a read as the train hurtles on through a maze of tunnels, passageways, and tubes at blazing speeds over and under rivers. Our car jerks from side to side as we sway in unison. From time to time the lights go out, but nobody minds. It happens all the time. The trains just scream on. Day and night, workdays, weekends, holidays, millions cram themselves into the subways because in New York City, that's the way you get there.

*

By 1937, America is in a deep depression. It hit New York especially hard. Tough, savvy people explore every conceivable way of making a living; they pursue every angle, ponder every possibility, investigate every machination. The problem is how can you make a buck? They are established, know the language and the ropes a lot better than Jacob Hugo. Still, he combs the papers every night, calls listings in his "Cherman" accent, writes long-winded, boring letters detailing his background and experience, and sometimes even goes in for interviews. But nothing! All he ever gets are sales jobs—peddling marginal products to over-stocked customers, and then only on commission—no advances or guarantees. Our front room is cluttered with the products he is trying to peddle. They remind us of his struggles—a rotary press to compact newspapers into fire logs—several leaky packages of soy bean meal which, so the labels announce, yield "All The Elements Of Abundant Life"—an oscillating leather belt on a flimsy metal hinge to sharpen used razor blades—a vibrating display case in the form of a shallow platform on which an advertiser can place small figurines that vibrate and gyrate in random circles once you plug the thing in. At seven every morning, with his sample case in one hand, his briefcase in the other, he leaves the house with subway maps and lists of prospective customers in his lapel pocket. And now and then he gets an order or two, but the commissions are small and late in coming. He tries writing—a novel and poetry—slaving over an ancient typewriter late into the night desperately hoping for some kind of breakthrough and still insists there has to be a way to make a living in America. But it eludes him. The best he ever does is to export California wines to a few of his former customers in Europe. Still, there is never enough money, and we are forced to move to a cheaper apartment a few blocks away on Fourth Avenue, a little bit smaller and a floor higher. That saves $10 a month.

In our new place you have to put quarters in the meters, one for electricity and one for gas, and it isn't unusual for the lights to go out in the middle of the evening and for somebody to have to run down three flights of stairs to feed the meter. And while there had been an abundance of cockroaches at 61st Street, they were nothing compared to our newest companions—bed bugs. Little, dark brown, button-like critters that swell up twice their size after they've tapped you. They leave you with a welt the size of a dime or bigger. If you ever squash one after it's been at you, you shudder at the oozing blood between your fingers. They're so totally resistant to bug spray and so good at hiding that Mother has us break down her bed and our couch every Saturday morning and dunk the corners of the frames into scalding water in the bathtub to chase them out of cracks and crevices. But her efforts make little difference. Rumor has it they hide in the ceiling and drop down on you at night.

Our ice box holds a 25 pound block of ice in the top

compartment. One time we forget to empty the melt from the pan underneath. Soon dripping water is discovered in the Western Union office on the ground floor of our building. They inquire on the first floor as to where the water is coming from, then the second and soon half of the residents of the building stand on the landing outside our front door giving us holy hell. It's all we can do to keep from being evicted.

Father smokes a pipe, Mother and brother cigarettes. Now and then I snitch a cigarette or two from her purse, but mainly I do what all the other kids do, pick up spit-soggy cigarette butts from off streets and subway platforms where smokers have dumped them. They make me dizzy and sick. As soon as I get past our front door, I head for the bathroom and brush my teeth furiously, but I'm sure they know—just don't say anything.

Sometimes at night when he isn't typing, he gets out his old cello and plays—Boccherini, Bach and Dvorak—just saws away like in the old days—totally lost.

As short of money as he is, he opens a $5 savings account for each of us, Fritz and me. It's an important thing for him to do—like a covenant, almost religious. I add a few cents to mine now and then. Often, a few of us kids hang around our only grocery store hoping a customer might need somebody to carry her bundles home—it might mean a few pennies or a nickel. One time, the shoe repair guy who leases a booth right across from the Western Union office in our building asks me if I want to make some money. Sure. Since he doesn't have a stitching machine for heavy leather, my job is to take three pairs of shoes in a large brown paper bag to his cousin's shop two miles down Fourth Avenue and get the soles stitched up. I return about two hours later, and he gives me two pennies for my trouble. But then in winter whenever it snows, sometimes kids like me get as much as a quarter for cleaning the snow off people's sidewalks.

Once, at dinner, it comes out that Dad has a swelling in his groin. It turns out to be a hernia. As time passes, the bulge gets bigger, and he orders a truss for $6.95 through a magazine ad. It's a big spring-like affair that has a pad in front which fits over the protruding intestine. He calls it his "Schweinerei" (pig mess) but tolerates it. An operation would cost over $100—impossible!

With increasing regularity on my way to school on Fourth Avenue, I see people actually living in the street—families who have been evicted. Not bums or hobos, but whole families huddled together on tattered couches or layers of cardboard in alleys and below-level revetments next to coal chutes. Where do they cook and eat I wonder—or change their clothes—or go to the bathroom? And how long do the owners and the police allow them there? And then what?

Fritz has always loved ships and boats—anything that floats. He gets the arrival and departure times of the big ocean liners out of the paper, and the two of us go down to the pier on 57th Street and watch the likes of the "Normandie," the "Amsterdam," or the "Hamburg" glide quietly in or out of the harbor. And we try our hand at fishing. No poles—just a skein of line, a lead sinker and some hooks. He sets bloody pieces of fish intestines on the hooks and brings in a couple of slithery eels that coil like snakes when he lands them. We dump them into a bucket filled with sea water and even land more than a dozen small pink crabs that won't let go of the bait even after you've pulled them out of the water. They too go into the bucket. When we get home, we dump the whole slithery mess into the bathtub, but somehow the crabs get out. Most of them crawl around our apartment, and we're able to retrieve them, but a few scramble down the ventilation shaft that connects all the bathrooms in the building. The eels are still in the tub when Mother goes in there. She lets out a scream you can hear clear down on Fourth Avenue. "Eine Schlange!" (a snake!) she hollers. Even months later we still hear talk from some of the neighbors about a crab or two being found in somebody's bathroom.

*

Luckily there is enough money to buy Mother an inexpensive hearing aid—a small black box that fits into the inside of her bodice with a little black wire that connects to a hearing aide in her ear. Hallelujah! Though there is a lot of crackling and squealing, she can hear so much better and consequently is better able to communicate with others. As a matter of fact, she starts doing piece work: knitting, crocheting, and applique. It takes weeks and weeks to complete one knitted dress. First the front of the blouse—often in two parts—then the back, then the sleeves and collar, and finally the skirt—a monumental task in itself—all knit on a long curved needle in one piece to avoid seams. Often, she finds a mistake and many days' work has to be ripped out. And when it is finally, finally finished and blocked and ironed and lovingly wrapped in tissue and boxed, it still only brings in at most thirteen, maybe fifteen dollars.

Once she sends me to the store with a ten dollar bill to buy groceries. In those days, the clerks, not the customers, retrieve the things you ask for. They mark down the price of each item on a brown paper bag, and it's fascinating to watch them add up your bill without the aid of an adding machine almost instantly, two columns at a time. Going back home, I hear loud sirens just around the corner, so I investigate. There are three fire engines—red lights flashing. Smoke is pouring out of a window three-quarters of the way up the side of a tall apartment house, people standing at an open window up there screaming to get down. Hurriedly, the firemen set their ladders up against the red brick wall next to the window and haul them out. I watch for about a half hour and start home, but to my utter horror realize that I either lost or somebody clipped three dollar bills, part of the change I got from the ten dollar bill my mother had given me—the coin change was still in my pocket. I'm petrified to go home. How can I ever, ever explain? How stupid and careless can you get? An idea. I go back to the grocery store, tell them what happened, and ask to borrow three dollars promising to repay the money since I had over eight dollars in the bank. To my great surprise, they agree and the next day, right after school, I withdraw the money from my bank and pay them back.

One night, Father brings home a small box that turns out to be a tiny Emerson radio. Pure magic. Every night at ten o'clock, they listen to the news with Hans von Kaltenborn, and on Sundays there are concerts with the likes of Thomas Beecham, Bruno Walter, Dimitri Metropolis and Arturo Toscanini conducting. On Saturdays, she never misses the Metropolitan Opera with Milton Cross. But me, I get to hear Jack Armstrong, "The All-American Boy," the Lone Ranger, One Man's Family, Little Orphan Annie, Dick Tracy, The Shadow, Buck Rogers, The Green Hornet, Uncle Don, Mayor La Guardia reading the Sunday funnies and, best of all, Red Barber, the voice of the Brooklyn Dodgers. And one night, with the volume real low and my ear right next to the speaker, I'm half scared out of my mind when Orson Wells presents "The War of the Worlds." Even though the announcer keeps telling us that it's only a drama, the broadcast is so realistic I keep looking out the window to see if the invaders from Mars have crossed the harbor yet on their way to our house in Brooklyn. It's reported that one person died of a heart attack that night while listening.

And often on Saturday afternoons some of us kids head down to the Varsity movie house on Sixth Avenue. It only costs 10 cents to get in—two main features, a cartoon, coming attractions, and the scariest serial ever. Episode Six: Dick Tracy is cornered by "The Hook" way up on a steel girder. Instead of a hand, this guy has a sharp metal hook. Tracy is trapped. If he steps back even one inch, he'll fall to his death. There is no way for him to get out, and we watch in horror as the villain takes careful aim at Tracy's skull, and with swelling chords of ominous music, we see the lethal hook come down with speed and force . . . And that's when the action stops. If you want to find out what happened, you have to come back next week. There is a matron present; she wears a white uniform like a nurse. To make room for new customers, if she thinks you've seen the show once already, she makes you get up and sit right down in the very front row where the sound is deafening and the images elongated and surreal . . . and you come out punch-drunk and cock-eyed.

At 12, I graduate from the sixth grade at P.S. 118 and start at Dewey Junior High School down about 20 blocks on Fourth Avenue. By now, I'm just about in the right grade for my age, and my all-time favorite is Miss Rowland, my 7th grade English

teacher. She is young and tall with a milk white complexion and shiny black hair combed back in a bun. She always wears low cut blouses, and you can see the separation between her abundant breasts when she bends over—which she does a lot. She is warm and fetching yet distant and professional all at the same time. First we do *The Lady of the Lake* and then *The Merchant of Venice*. And when she pretends to be Portia and reads to us, she drips with compassion. How could you turn her down?
"The quality of mercy is not strain'd,
It droppeth as the gentle rain from heaven . . ."
Still I have mixed emotions. In its day, true, a Jew named Shylock was the villain of the play—ah, but not so fast says Shakespeare. After all, the poor guy was driven to his madness by so much hatred and prejudice against him. On my way home from school, I think about all this a lot, and that night make up my mind that I will tell Miss Rowland and the whole class. But it just so happens that the next day, one of my last baby teeth comes loose, and I have this compulsion to wiggle it back and forth determined to get it out. "Franz, will you stop bothering that tooth," she scolds, really annoyed. I feel terrible. To get a rebuff from Miss Rowland is simply awful. Immediately I take my finger out of my mouth and close my lips, but still can't resist pushing the damned thing back and forth with my tongue—and lo and behold—it pops out. When she isn't looking, I spit it into my hand, and for a moment imagine I am Shylock delivering his famous speech:
"I am a Jew. Hath not a Jew eyes? Hath not a Jew hands, organs, dimensions, senses, affections, passions?" I taste the sweet ooze from the gap in my gum and look at that tiny tooth, "And if you pluck out our teeth, do we not bleed?"
And it's not as though there weren't a lot of other Jew-haters in America—people like Henry Ford, Charles Lindberg and Father Coughlin who comes on the radio every Sunday night with an hour-long anti-Semitic rant. Worse yet is Fritz Kuhn, head of the German American Bund. He's always decked out in his brown-shirt Nazi uniform with Swastikas fluttering all around as he boasts of having more than 20,000 paying members in his organization.

All these folks are overjoyed when in 1936 Max Schmeling comes over from Germany and knocks out Joe Louis, and thrilled when the dirigible "Hindenburg" makes it across the Atlantic to Lakehurst, New Jersey. But then when it explodes the following year, and Louis wins the re-match in '38, I feel like maybe the Nazis aren't so invincible after all.

They have what they call a knot-hole club at junior high. You pay a quarter and get to go to two Brooklyn Dodger games. I am surprised about Ebbets Field, how small it is, at least from the outside, a kind of high round construction right next to the street. Scores of kids without tickets are climbing the high wire fence in back of the grandstands trying to sneak in—all in plain view of the mounted policemen who ride over and make them get down. But the game is wonderful. Leo Durocher, their feisty manager, gets into a big fight with the umpires and the Dodgers win. I dramatize it all with great hyperbole to my friends on our block. But the second time I go, the game is sold out, and I can't get in. Since I had done so much bragging about going, I hang around a hot dog stand in front of the stadium that has the radio going and listen to Red Barber describe the game. After it's over, I join the crowd headed toward the subway, pretend like I had been there, and tell them all about it.

Often on my way to and from school, the boys match chewing gum cards. These are 3 by 3 inch cards you get when you buy a flat piece of pink bubble gum for a penny. They all have war pictures on them—atrocities committed by Japanese soldiers in their war with China—children bayoneted, civilians bombed, bloody limbs and heads flying off bodies. And there are dirty cards as well; the kids call them "bibles." One guy throws his card down and the other tries to match it—heads or tails. Having practiced over and over, the second guy holds his card just so, swings his arm and lets go precisely at the bottom of his arc so that the card will tumble to the ground just as he wants, heads or tails. If it's a match, he gets to keep both cards; if not, he loses his.

And nearby, the girls are forever jumping rope to the rhythm of a never-ending sing-song jingle . . .

"Lulu had a baby,
She named him Tiny Tim;
Put him in a piss-pot
To teach him how to swim . . .
He swam to the bottom,
He swam to the top,
Lulu got excited,
And grabbed him by his . . .
Cock-tail, ginger ale, five cents a glass,
If you don't like it,
You can shove it up your . . . "
On and on.

And then somehow a toy that looked like a small wooden spool gets to be the rage with all of us kids. The call it a "yo-yo." One end of a string loops around its axle while you tie the other end to your finger. You wind up the string and throw it down. It spins so fast going down that it has enough momentum to wind itself up again right back into your hand. And every week or so a guy with a New York accent who says he's an Hawaiian yo-yo champ comes around and organizes a block-wide yo-yo contest. After showing off what he can do, he tells us that the winner of the contest will get a real 'stay-down' yo-yo like the ones he sells. Well, since most of us have been practicing all week, now is our chance to prove what we can do. But getting that yo-yo to do tricks isn't all that easy. Just making it stay down and do what they call "walking the dog" is hard enough, and it's only when you can do advanced tricks like "rock the baby in the cradle," or "fly around the moon," that you have a chance of winning something.

*

Meanwhile, Father finally has to go see somebody about his hernia. The doctor tells him it's so big now that it could fold over on itself, block his intestines and kill him. So he borrows $125 and admits himself to a hospital in Brooklyn. He's supposed to be out in a week, but contracts an infection. They have him in a large ward of men—a tiny pale figure with tubes draining from his groin. Still he keeps his briefcase next to his bed and writes letters to potential customers. Before he entered the hospital, he had sold some wine to the Swedish Monopole—in those days their government ran the liquor stores over there—and now the order needs processing. So he carefully gives me instructions, point by point: First go to the wine company in Manhattan, get them to make out the invoices, the bills of lading and the insurance forms; take all those to the custom house, then to the Holland America line which is the shipping agent, and finally turn everything back into the wine company. It all goes well; he's pleased. I just turned 14 and feel very grown up. It means $125 for us, money we desperately need to pay bills. But the trouble is that he isn't getting any better—just lies there week after week.

Fritz graduates from high school with honors. He's awarded a beautiful medal with a diamond chip in it for superior scholarship, and though at first they didn't admit him into the City College of New York because he's an alien, he finally made it to college and got himself a part-time job working in the newspaper room of the big public library in Manhattan. With Father in the hospital, Fritz's earnings make all the difference. Without them, we can't survive.

Mother hears about a place that needs seamstresses to do shoulder pads, and we call right away. Yes, they have work—lots of it they tell us—but you need a sewing machine. Sure, we tell 'em, we have one—which is a lie. The place is on the twelfth floor of an office building right in the heart of the garment district in Manhattan—cluttered and busy. The clerk sends me home with two large cardboard boxes filled with black rayon shoulder pad halves, spools of black binding tape and a mountain of cotton. The minute I get home, Mother and I buy a used table top sewing machine for $18—six dollars down, two a week. First you sew the two halves of the pad together, shiny side in—like sausages—dozens and dozens. These get turned inside out, stuffed with cotton, and sewed up with binder tape. We sew and sew late into the night. Getting the binding right is tough even with a binder guide attachment because you're sewing through four layers of material. Stitches knot up and needles break; the leather belt from the motor slips because there's too much resistance, and then the motor overheats; meanwhile, the bobbin gets stuck and the tension goes haywire. And even after we finish, there is the cat and mouse game I have to play with the subway guards who don't allow people with big cartons like that on trains. But even at $1.75 a gross, we do pretty well for about five weeks.

And then one afternoon, as I lift two boxes of finished work up on to his counter, the receiving clerk, whose accent is even thicker than mine, hands me a postcard and tells me to write my name and address on it. "Ve send you ven ve get da voik," he says. Of course, we never hear from him again and have to take the sewing machine back.

A couple of weeks later, Father finally makes it home, weak and thin. He immediately starts to try to sell again—canvassing, phoning, calling on potential customers. But then one day as he's up at the wine company, just out of the blue, the boss, who is the son of the winery owner in California, calls him into his office and tells him that if he wants it, he can have a bookkeeping job on a big grape ranch in California—$80 a month and a house to live in <u>free!</u>

"Imagine, imagine!" he's ecstatic. "Can you imagine such a thing? Over our heads, a real roof, for nothing. For absolutely nothing! Never again to worry about the verdamnte rent. Never again to worry about being evicted. Besides, with the war coming, there'll probably be no more wine sales overseas."

Fritz doesn't want to go because he's in college and has a job—makes enough to get by. But I want to go. California sounds great to me—open spaces, real land, oranges, a farm where you can grow things, a place to get out into nature and breathe fresh air, away from cramped apartment buildings, paved-over everything, crowded subways, evictions, and this everlasting, nerve wracking, insecurity about money. "Don't hesitate for a minute," I tell them. "Go, go!" I beg them. And they decide to do it—YES! Good, I'm glad. We'll go—the three of us—Fritz will come later.

Once again Mother carefully packs the few surviving treasures from the old days—four embroidered linen sheets and pillow cases, a pre-WW I engraved silver tea and coffee set, six tiny silver monogrammed dessert spoons, and several paintings, one of which is a portrait of herself painted some 25 years ago. All of it goes into the same steamer trunk that brought it across the Atlantic.

The rent has been paid till the end of May, and that is the exact day, Memorial Day 1939, that we board a dowdy Greyhound bus, and the driver punches our tickets. It would take three and a half days to get from Brooklyn to Madera, California.

*

Norm

fiction

Already late, I rushed out of the heat and glaring sunlight into the chapel. For a moment everything went dark—hard to see—but the sound of the hurdy-gurdy organ left no doubt where I was. An usher pressed a program in my hand and hustled me into a seat in the last row of the center aisle. The service was already under way.

As my eyes adjusted, I realized the small hall was packed—most everybody from work. I was actually surprised that there weren't more people from beyond the work circle.

And then I was thinking—'Isn't this just like Norm's last cabinet meeting with us?' I opened the little folded program—green curlicue printing on white paper—Norm's last handout to us. Here, he tells us in that flat, sarcastic, biting voice of his are my vital statistics, and these are my survivors, and here are the people who are officiating at my last appearance above ground, and that's the way it ends. So don't ask, and don't tell, and don't concern yourself about it no more because the ballgame is over. On the back of the program was a sentimental little poem he would have hated.

And it occurred to me that most of us will probably do with this mushy little folded program what we did with just about all the other hand-outs he gave us over the years—dump it.

Bonnie is up front, all in black. It was she, most everybody agrees, for whom he worked so hard, for whom he wanted to excel and prove so much, and for whom, now at last, he hadn't really succeeded.

A prayer.

And the minister asks for silent meditation "to remember Norman," and I don't know what to think. He often harassed and angered me. Just a big, pig-headed jock—the exact opposite of what I always thought an educator ought to be like . . . "But speak nothing but good of the dead," says the proverb. Still, I'm confused and troubled.

Most school people work for years and years—probably beyond their usefulness. Their lecture notes turn to crinkly yellow and their skins to leather. Though they might resist it, sooner or later, there is no escaping the obligatory retirement dinner replete with flowery speeches and a plaque to hang up on the wall. Then, perhaps a cruise to Alaska or the grand tour of Europe up the Rhine to try out the new camcorder they got for Christmas. And finally, they settle down and join the retired teachers' club they call "The Emeriti." Some even teach a class or two at adult school or write sage and weighty letters to the editor. But sooner or later, good brother time wins his inevitable foot race, and they too tread gently into that good night.

Not Norm. He never tread gently into nothing. God, I just talked to him a few days ago—sucking on a Camel as usual—jumpy and nervous. And that very evening, while driving home from work, he collapsed over the wheel of his car as it jumped the curb, clipped a fire hydrant and skidded to a stop across some people's lawn. A couple of motorists saw it all and tried to revive him. But it was all over. A massive heart attack at 56.

*

Well over six feet, husky, with a barrel chest, a closely cropped crew cut, and broad shoulders, Norm could easily double for the most intimidating bodyguard. He'd been a collegiate football player as well as a boxer, had suffered a trick knee that might pop out on occasion from the former and a flat, oft-broken nose from the latter.

Everybody knew no one showed up earlier or stayed later than Norman, that he pushed and drove himself doggedly and mercilessly. A chain smoker and heavy drinker, his hair-trigger temper was set to explode at the slightest provocation. Always double-timing it like when he was in the Army Rangers during his infantry days, Norm kept up his grueling pace with unrelenting discipline. Forever hurrying, rushing, and pressing, he was the human definition of perpetual motion. In all the years I worked with this guy, I never saw him when he didn't have a crucial task to complete, an urgent deadline to meet, a couple of emergencies to deal with, or some frenzied, last minute catching-up to do. If there wasn't a real crisis, Norm manufactured one. He was forever wiping the sweat off his face, always out of breath, always short-tempered and cranky as he spent his days frantically racing on the treadmill he had fashioned for himself.

Some believed he set it up that way, his feverish pace and whirlwind-activity, as a badge of martyrdom. Maybe he wanted people to say, "Oh, look at Norman . . . Look how hard he works; how much he accomplishes, and what little credit he gets for all he does."

He had wanted to go into combat during the World War, but because of the knee, they made an infantry training officer out of him at a base way out in the desert. I often heard him tell about how he pounded those "whiny, grubby, dog-faces" up and down and across the company square no matter what the temperature, and how he double-timed them through barren sand dunes til they dropped of exhaustion.

In my very first semester at the college, one of my students suffered an epileptic seizure. There he lay, unconscious, frothing at the mouth, his body shaking and shuddering uncontrollably. I ran down the hall and called the nurse, but since they had her working half days at a high school across town, Norman himself, then the assistant to the Dean of Student Services, ran over. He charged into the room like a half-back on an end-around, and without a word to anyone, jumped on the student, straddled him like a wrestler and started pulling his arms away from his body. We looked on anxiously as the two of them contested for supremacy. With instinctive strength, the unconscious student tried to pull his arms and legs together into a prenatal crouch while Norm fought for the exact opposite, determined to spread-eagle the guy. We all hoped the encounter wouldn't last too long. I felt like the class wanted me to say something to Norman, to intervene with him on behalf of the student, but I didn't dare. Thank goodness, the student came around shortly. For a time he moaned and groaned but finally woke. We got him some water and made pillows and blankets out of jackets and coats.

"How ya doin'?" I asked.

"Okay, I guess," he replied, still groggy. "I . . . I'm sorry . . . I . . ."

"Please, please. Don't even think about it," I tried to reassure him. "Sure you're okay?"

"I . . . I feel so exhausted . . . my arms and shoulders are so sore and spent . . . Oh . . ." He folded his arms across his chest.

"I'm not surprised," I told him. "After all, you just went six rounds with our version of King Kong."

Norm was already long gone.

*

He had more years here at the college than any other administrator. As a matter of fact, Norm came with the place when it was converted from a high school to a junior college. At the high school, he'd been the football coach and later, the director of athletics. After a few years at the college, they promoted him to become the Dean of Student Services.

When you're a new teacher like me, they always sign you up for some flunky job besides your teaching, and that's how I got to supervise the sales of programs at football and basketball games — a job I couldn't shake for about three years. So that after each game I headed up to the announcer's booth where Norman and I would count all the receipts from the box office, the refreshment stand, and the program sales and zip them into a green bank bag which he locked up in the safe they had up there to be picked up and deposited later. And then the two of us would close up the announcer's booth, the dressing and bathrooms, and turn off the stadium lights.

And once in a while, he'd invite me over to the Golden Ant Hill, a honky-tonk joint where all the coaches and referees hung-out after the weekend games. Norm always started off by downing a couple of boiler makers. "Just to catch up," he'd tell me. Up went the shot glass as he swallowed hard. "Aaah," he grimaced and shook his head a couple of times. "That'll clear your sinuses for you."

They all sat around a big table in the back, ordered pitchers of beer and rehashed all the big plays of the night—who won, who lost, who was upset, who were the heroes, who the villains, and who got screwed? And one night, they got into a heated argument about the new curriculum at East High—a school which had dropped its P.E. requirement for graduation—insisted that the athletes on all teams take more academic classes—and added a new subject to their curriculum, some dippy thing they called 'conflict resolution.' Everybody was heatedly talking about it when Norm, pretty well loaded by now, stood up, hit the table hard with the flat of his hand, and hollered, "That kind of stuff is a lot of bullshit, and we all know it . . . In order to survive, a male human being, you know—a real man—has to be a warrior, a guy who uses his dukes—let's leave the damn women out a' this," he stormed. "I don't care what anybody says; that's the only way you can be a real man. You hear what I'm sayin?—Now if you're an artsy fartsy fagpot or a pimply-faced poetry major or a f - - - n' ballet daisy, well, how the hell can you ever be a real man anyway? . . . The answer is you f - - - n' can't. What a man does in this life is hustle and compete and scrounge and snooty-pooch the ladies, right? . . . and sports is where you learn it . . . P.E. is your apprenticeship. Right, Thad?" he looked right at me. "Because if you can't hunt and kill like you do in war, you do the next best thing; you get out there on that football field and kick the livin' crap out of whoever the hell gets in your f - - - n' way. Right?"

They had this on-going contest about who could urinate the longest. And whenever somebody who'd been sopping up beer all night thought he was 'ready,' they'd send him out to the john with a monitor and the official stop watch which the bartender kept under the counter for them.

And after a while, Norm announced that he was ready, and he and another guy went in. The other guy came back to the table, but out of the corner of my eye, I could see Norm head over to the bar, pick up the phone and talk a while. Soon he came back with a whole tray of beer and several tubs of popcorn.

About that time, two of the regulars, Sanderson and Kovic,

returned from the state high school basketball championship held in a nearby city. Sanderson had been the head referee, and the big joke was that Kovic got into the game free by telling the guy at the gate that he had to drive the head referee over because the poor son of a bitch couldn't see well enough to get a driver's license.

"Oh, sure, sir," Kovic mimicked the ticket taker bowing in a courtly fashion. "Sure, sir. Come right in, sir." Everybody roared. "It's so nice of you to drive the poor blind bastard over here." More laughter.

I looked at my watch. It was 1:30 in the morning. What a waste of time I thought! Time to shove off. Oh, what the hell, I'll try it one more time. So I told them I was ready to go for the record before I took off. "Me too," said Sanderson. They gave us the stop watch and told us we were on our honor, and we both peed into the same filthy bowl as the stop watch ticked away.

When we got back, a woman was sitting next to Norm. Obviously Hispanic, her glossy black hair was combed straight back in a bun. He never introduced her, but I noticed his arm was around the back of her—real low—and one of her legs was draped across the top of his knee.

*

The next year I became the debate coach. Whenever a competition took us out of town, I had to go through Norm to get transportation. Believe me, he made you jump through hoops. Our schedule had to be approved way ahead of time, and each trip request had to be signed off in triplicate by a bunch of administrators. And what infuriated me the most was that he let the jocks get just about anything they wanted anytime without hardly any approvals at all. All they had to do was call Norm and damn near on a moment's notice some dink could get the best station wagon in the fleet just to go scout another team.

One Sunday night, after getting back late from a trip with the team, I couldn't find the school's credit card. Believe me, I searched everywhere—high and low—inside, outside—my clothes, my wallet, my briefcase, the station wagon—but no luck. The thought of having to tell Norman that I lost the school's credit card kept me awake til past midnight. In desperation I searched out the phone number of the last service station where we had bought gas and called them. Thank God! They found it—right where I left it—on top of the container that housed the windshield towels. By now, it was sitting safely in their cash register. Sure, they would mail it to us. No problem. Man, what a relief!

*

"You did what?" he howled, his voice echoing through the office for everybody to hear.

"I left it at the service station, Norm . . . Look, I'm sorry. It was late, and I simply forgot it after I cleaned the windshield . . . but it's okay, Norm. They found it . . . they're gonna mail it."

"What a dumb-ass, stupid thing to do," he bellowed, his jet black eyes boring holes into me. "What the hell am I supposed to do if someone needs it today? And what if they don't mail it?"

"It'll get here, Norman," I pleaded . . . "I'm sure it'll get here . . . Look, I'm sorry . . . They'll mail it to us. After all, we're good customers."

He just stood up and stuck a Camel in his mouth, "Well, the next time, why don't you just take your own damned car," he snapped as he lit up, clicked his Zippo shut, and dashed out the door.

The following year, we were fortunate enough to have two of our debate teams (four students) qualify for the state finals—a singular honor our school had never experienced before. So at a quarter to five in the morning, with four kids and all their junk waiting, and with a two and a half hour trip ahead of us, here I am trying to open the padlock to the car barn gate, but somehow the key Norm had given me wouldn't work. In the semi-darkness, I wiggled, jiggled, cajoled, fussed and cussed that stupid key. In desperation, even asked the students to try. No luck. That key simply would not turn the damned lock—and time was slipping away.

So I drove my car over to a public phone, looked up Norm's home phone number and dialed. Bonnie answered. I told her of my predicament, but she wasn't about to wake Norm.

"Norman's been up half the night ill," she told me. "He just drifted off a half hour ago. He desperately needs his rest," she insisted. "I wouldn't wake him for anything."

"But Bonnie, look, I've got to get these kids to their competition on time. This is the state meet. They only have it once a year. It's a two and a half hour drive from here. These kids have worked so hard for this—for months and months, practically all year."

No response.

"Bonnie? Bonnie, are you there? I'm really in a bind here. Look, you've got to help me out here."

"I told you, I'm not waking him for nobody," she repeated.

"But Bonnie . . ."

"Norman does enough for you people over there at that college. Nobody ever appreciates the things he does anyway," she blurted out and bang! Hung up.

About a half hour later, we were finally able to flag down a janitor who let us into the car barn, but arrived a good hour late to the competition, the students thoroughly pissed of course—me too. The delay absolutely crippled our chances of winning anything because each of our teams had to take a "no show" in their first round.

It turned out that Norm had given me the wrong key—the stupid jerk—a fact he never acknowledged or apologized for. Had anybody done that to him, he would have had them boiled in oil.

*

A few years later, guess what? I became an administrator myself—an Associate Dean of Instruction—and that's when I saw yet another side of Norman. In all the meetings we attended, he always stuck up for the head man, the President. Just like in the army, always loyal to the chain of command—probably because he, himself, wanted to move up in it.

And maybe that's why they had him doing just about everything for that college—business manager, adviser to student government and activities, in charge of transportation, manager of the bookstore and the cafeteria—even in charge of the maintenance crew. It was Norm who drove over in the middle of the night to fix the boiler or repair the sprinkler system. It was Norm they blamed when the noodle casserole in the cafeteria was too soupy or the price of textbooks too high.

We all believed he worked so hard because he wanted to get ahead—because he had ambition. After all, as Dean of Student Services he was just a few steps away from the presidency. That's why he put his shoulders to the wheel so that Bonnie, the daughter of a major and a strict believer in the officer class, could realize her dream of one day hosting the President's tea.

One morning he burst into my office past our secretary, carrying a stack of cafeteria trays that had paint smeared all over them. "Those art flakes of yours are using our cafeteria trays to mix their paints on," he roared. "Here," he fumed and dropped the whole stack on my desk with a loud crash. "See what you can do, Dean! . . . You ARE the DEAN, ain'tchoo?" he taunted.

And even though he already had so many responsibilities, somehow he always seemed to get picked on to do even more and more—most of it just flunky, two-bit stuff. And what was so demeaning was that it usually happened when everyone was around to see and observe, like in cabinet—as though the President wanted to push Norm's nose into it in public. One afternoon, since the regular secretary wasn't there to take minutes, he asked Norm to take them. And then, in the space of not more than five minutes, he asked him to see about changing the hours of the bookstore because some students had complained, requested that he find out what our policy was concerning the donation of books, musical instruments, and works of art, and asked him to check with the district office about our latest enrollment figures. We could see he was doing a slow burn while all this was coming down. So that he answered stiff through clenched teeth. "Yeah, and if I stick a broom up my ass, I can sweep the halls while I'm doin' all this runnin' around!" Loud and prolonged laughter even from the women. But the President made out like he hadn't heard, and I saw Norm wince, clutch his shoulder hard, quickly reach in his shirt pocket, and pop a pill.

*

Every year, all of us administrators go on a weekend retreat up to a resort in the mountains. We usually leave on Friday around noon and get back Saturday night late. Officially it's billed as "In-service Training," but I always get the feeling it's more like a medieval fealty ceremony, his royal highness wanting to know if all the lords and ladies were still paying attention—still laughing at the right jokes.

To Norm, it must have been a sign of his decline since he was assigned to room with me. In the past, he always got assigned to travel and room with a full Dean, not an "associate" like me.

So he drove the two of us up in a school station wagon in almost total silence. And the absolute first thing he did when we arrived, he hurriedly went into the little store next to the lodge where we were staying, bought a fifth of whiskey and a six pack of beer, and spent the next hour drinking boiler makers—not that he ever got drunk—just raw and ugly. Our first administrators' meeting started at four, and the two of us sat together. He said nothing, just smoked continuously while sneaking belts from the bottle inside a wrinkled brown paper bag hidden in the folds of his overcoat which lay crumpled in his lap.

Later that evening, during the happy hour before dinner, a couple of administrators walked up to where we were sitting.

"Norm, see those two blondes over there at the bar?" one nodded in their direction. "Norm, they're on the town, baby . . . Fifty dollars, Norm . . . either one of 'em will screw your brains out for fifty dollars."

Groggy in the smoke and haze, he never said a word, just lit another Camel, snapped his Zippo shut, and stared at me. I could see his mind wander back to his Ranger days and those long nights at the Golden Ant Hill. Finally, the warrior jock raised his head and inhaled the musky bloom of the evening.

"Where are they?" he grunted.

"Right over there," one of them nodded in their direction, "the ones with the big boobs and tight jeans."

He stood up, flared his nostrils, and shuffled over.

And got in about five the next morning. Couldn't get the

door to our room open, so he slid open the window from the verandah outside and crashed head first onto the floor inside. He never came down for breakfast and missed the whole morning session. Since the President had us pick up manila folders with our names on them, he knew exactly who had ditched the meeting by who hadn't picked up their folder—a fact, we all knew he duly noted, especially in Norm's case.

*

A couple months later, one of our art teachers forgot to requisition the all-purpose room where she had planned to put on a demonstration of paper making. With only a couple of days before the event, she wanted me to intercede with Norman so she could get the room.

"Oh, man," I moaned. "Do you know what you're asking? That request should have been turned in months and months ago."

"Oh, dear. I know. I know," she said. "I'm so sorry, Dean. But we've advertised all over town already; hundreds of people tell us they're coming. All the food and punch has been ordered. Dean, please! You've got to help me out this time."

"All right, all right. I'll see what I can do."

*

On my way over to see Norman, I tried to figure out the best way to approach him. But when I got there, he already had someone in his office.

"It'll be just a minute," said Mrs. Henry, his secretary. "Would you like a cup of coffee while you're waiting?"

"Sure," I told her, and she poured one in a Styrofoam cup. Before I knew it, Norm was free, and she told me to go ahead in.

"Norm," I said, walking through the door, "I gotta talk to you about one of our art people puttin' on a demonstration this weekend in the all-purpose room. We expect lots of people to show up."

"Look," he snapped, "don't bring that coffee in here!"

"What?" I didn't understand.

"You heard me," he commanded. "That's all they want to do out there is drink coffee at their desks, and I've already told them no. They're not to drink coffee at their work stations. And now I don't want it to look like I allow coffee drinking in here when I don't allow it out there."

"Norm, you're kidding?"

"Oh, no, I'm not . . . Not kidding at all . . . especially when they all can see."

"God, man, why don't you chill out, Norman," I said laughing. "Honestly, I think you're cracking up! Look, this is one time we'll just not let them see, okay?" So I stepped over to the side of his desk. "Lookie here," I said, "let's just set this little, ittie bittie coffee cup right down here behind the big telephone—like this—okay? . . . There. Now nobody from out there can possibly see it, right?"

"But, I . . ."

"Norman! Nobody can see the goddamned coffee cup for Chris sake! For once in your life, will you just f - - - n' relax?"

He let it go, and I got started filling out the requisition for the all-purpose room when the phone rang . . . Oh, No-o-o-o!

The instant I heard that thing ring, I knew exactly what was going to happen—as though I were clairvoyant and could see every single detail of the nightmare that was about to ensue. Still, I was totally paralyzed, as though in a trance, powerless—could not move a finger or speak a word—totally helpless—just looked on in horror as the nightmare continued.

As soon as Norm brought the receiver to his ear, the phone's cord which had been curled around my coffee cup, caught it at its base, and—SLOSH!—over it went. A whole cup of hot coffee propelled itself across his desk. A glistening spear of steaming liquid tan zipped like a dagger over and around several piles of paper and began dripping over the front of his desk right into an open drawer crammed full of hanging files. For a moment he was silent, just stared at the wall, seemingly speechless. Then he screamed "Jesus!" at the top of his voice and went mute again. I didn't wait for an encore—just high-tailed it to the nearest bathroom and brought back two fists full of paper towels and started sopping and mopping.

When I finally left his office that morning, the secretaries were all smirking, eyes twinkling—but not a word.

*

Just a few weeks ago, an anti-Vietnam war student group, enraged by an editorial in our student newspaper, decided they would shut the paper down. Norm heard of their plans, called me, and the two of us hustled over. The students, in a really ugly mood by now, looked like they were ready to storm the entrance to the newspaper office.

And while I was trying to call the police, Norman planted himself right in the middle of the front door of that office and faced them square on.

"If you people want to get in here, you're going to have to kick a lung out of me first!" he told them with unmistakable conviction. "One student," he declared. "One student can go in. Who is your President? If he isn't here, just pick one person to be your spokesman . . . That's right. One student and your adviser if he's around . . . and NOBODY ELSE. Now who's it gonna be?" he insisted.

Caught off balance, they selected one of their number, and though the meeting that ensued was long and stormy, it cleared the air with the parties reaching a fragile understanding. No question about it, without Norman, things would have ended up in a disaster that afternoon. That was his finest hour.

*

As the service progressed, you couldn't avoid seeing the American flag draped over the casket behind some floral sprays. Norman was under there—completely still now—not running anywhere to head off a crisis. My eyes glistened. God damn! I'm really gonna miss you—you stupid, super jock-ass jerk!— I wiped my eyes.

*

Once the service was over, everyone queued up to speak to Bonnie.

"I'm sorry," I told her and hugged her stiffly.

"That man was always there for you guys, from the very

beginning, wasn't he, Thad?"

"Yeah, from the very beginning, Bonnie. Nobody worked harder. We'll sure miss him."

"He sacrificed himself for that college, didn't he?" she said, raising her voice—"And they just crapped all over him, didn't they, Thad?"

I could see the tears forming in her eyes. "Humiliated and demeaned him at every turn," she went on. "Hell, I don't care who knows it—'cause it's true!"

I tried to calm her. "Everybody at the college appreciates what he did for us, Bonnie," I said as I clumsily embraced her a second time.

"We'll miss him, Bonnie," I repeated, and stepped aside to let the next person in line talk to her.

*

Madera

creative non-fiction

We pass around the thin Rand McNally gazetteer Father bought at the bus depot in New York. Madera, California,—just about in the center of the state, both from top to bottom and side to side. The county it's in produces cattle, alfalfa, cotton, fruit, grapes, lumber. There is a picture of an old car driving through the base of a giant redwood. I follow our route on the map. Right now we're in Pennsylvania, green and lush. He lights up a cigar even though the sign says no smoking. I sit next to him blowing the smoke to one side so that the driver won't notice.

Mother sits across the aisle from us knitting, glum and silent. I sense her mind: for the second time, the wandering Jews are forced to roam the earth to God knows where—among God knows whom. All because that gutter snipe, that uncultured street brawler, that latrine painter, that brutal, murdering fanatic demagogue Adolf Hitler has willed it. She clicks off her hearing aid and retreats into her all-encompassing rage—resigned to sit alone in hollow deafness—not much interested in where the bus is heading—stolid and sour—doggedly working her misery into the dress she's knitting.

America is flying by—so vast it takes a powerful, rumbling diesel like that with its throttle wide open three and a half days to get from sea to shining sea. City after city, town after town, state after state, mile after mile, the bus drones on over a seemingly inexhaustible ribbon of asphalt. The United States of America—an unbelievable, limitless abundance of just about everything.

On the morning of the fourth day, as we leave L.A. going north, we know it will take only a few more hours, and the looking becomes intense. Once past Bakersfield, I keep hoping for some mountains or at least maybe a hill or two, but there are only desolate farms way off into the hazy distance on both sides of the highway. Contrary to what I had expected, there is no golden glow, no orange hue, no verdant opulence. The San Joaquin Valley is flat, denuded, arid and monotonous, and the bus is getting hot. When the driver leans forward, I notice the back of his shirt is soaked. Father had changed into his only suit in the bathroom in L. A—a shop-worn blue gabardine—because he wants to make an impression. Then takes off his coat; still the sweat pours off him.

We arrive at about 1:30 in the afternoon, and our bus stops in an alley next to a small bus depot. The driver helps us off. The sign reads "Madera, Population 7,520," and it's sweltering hot. We stand on the soft blacktop next to the bus which is idling, gurgling out its smelly exhaust as the driver unloads our luggage. The sun is so bright, you have to squint to see. It beats down from above and radiates up off the ground. So we walk over into the merciful shade of the tiny bus depot with its single ticket window, small freight counter, and truncated soda fountain as the ceiling fan rotates lazily around a strip of yellow fly paper heavy with dead flies. The thermometer on the wall registers 98.

Mother glowers at me in pain. "My God, so boiling I am! Such a heat!" she scowls—an exclamation I would hear many times in the years to come. She gives her husband a pitiful look. "Ach, so eine Glut," she tells him. But he straightens up, shakes his glistening bald head, "Nah, ja . . . of course, a little hot it has to be, nicht wahr? Otherwise, how can there be sugar in the grapes for the wine, no?" But she doesn't answer. "Look," he says, "It's not all that bad now, eh? I mean, I don't feel nothing so terrible." to which the tall thin man behind the counter replies laconically, "Oh, this ain't nothin' yet, folks. It's only early June." He picks up his live cigarette from the edge of the counter and takes a drag. "Wait till we get into July, August and September. Whew! Last year, we had two weeks in a row all over 105—some days even over 110."

And nobody from the ranch has come to pick us up as he had eagerly expected inasmuch as he had written them. So we sit at the counter, and he orders apple pie and Cokes. I notice how old and strained they look—he, in that ill-fitting, baggy suit, wearing a dress shirt and a limp tie with a tie pin made from a real ancient coin in the likeness of the Roman Emperor Hadrian, a memento from their old days in Germany, and she with her red hair turning white, her expression sour, her lipstick uneven and partially smeared on her false teeth, forever fussing with the volume of her squealing hearing aid.

After waiting for almost an hour, he calls the ranch, and it takes another hour and a half before a faded green flat-bed Chevy truck arrives. The driver smilingly introduces himself as Manuel. He is a big, burly, friendly Mexican guy with a pug nose and thick black, curly hair. He helps us hoist our luggage up onto the truck bed.

"Whazat?" he asks, pointing to the cello, "a baby base? Hey, we could use one of those in the band."

"It's a cello," I offer. "Belongs to my father."

"Can he play *rancheras* or *paso dobles*?"

"I don't know, but I don't think so."

I help them into the dusty, tattered cab, slam the door closed, and swing myself onto the back of the truck where I sit right on the bed amid our luggage and some unfamiliar tools and machinery, cradling the cello in my lap. In just a few minutes we're beyond Madera's city limits and out in the country. We pass orchards, vineyards, cotton and alfalfa fields, pastures with horses and cattle grazing, and in about twenty minutes come to a long dirt road lined with tall palm trees on either side—the entrance to the ranch. The truck plows through powdery silt raising a cream-colored plume of dust in its wake. Beyond the palms, on both sides of the road, there is a never ending sea of deep green grapevines clear to the horizon. And suddenly, the 'home ranch' looms up ahead. A massive barn dwarfs all the other structures that surround it. Soon we're driving among the ranch buildings, and I begin to realize how old and dilapidated this place is. The raunchy sides of all the buildings are made up of old, mostly cracked, fading red vertical boards topped off with sagging green shingled roofs.

The driver makes a sharp turn just beyond the tall water tower. He shuts off his motor, and we coast to a stop with the faint squeal of his brakes. So this is it—our new home—the reason for us leaving New York—the 'free roof over our heads' along with $80 a month about which my father had been so euphoric. Though small and ramshackle, it sits beneath several tall eucalyptus trees which, I calculate, will grant us valuable shade. But before unloading, Manuel gives us a tour. There is a large kitchen with a smoke-smudged wood stove up against the interior wall, two bedrooms, and an unspeakably filthy bathroom that can only be accessed through the front porch. If you need hot water, he explains, you have to make a fire in the wood stove which, he shows us, has pipes—"coils" he calls them—circling the inside of the firebox. But who would ever want to make a fire when the temperature is already a hundred degrees?

Since it's too late to prepare supper, he invites us to eat in the cookhouse, family style, with about twenty ranch hands. Their silent bronzed faces are several shades darker than their balding scalps. They look tired and eye us politely. Underdone spareribs in tepid tomato sauce with beans, bread, margarine and coffee.

And so that night we sleep in California for the first time on three soiled mattresses on metal cots on loan from the bunkhouse. Early the next morning, I take a look around. The huge barn and its attached corral still dominate. I count 34 mules. Big reddish-brown beasts with long shifting ears and graying nostrils. They crowd together in front of a long trough, swishing their tails nervously, pull alfalfa through the tines, anxious to get a last mouthful before a long day out in the fields hitched to plows, vineyard wagons, sulfur dusters, hay mowers and manure spreaders. Just west of the barn is the bunkhouse where the ranch hands stay. It contains a long row of rooms, each with four cots in them, that face a long extended screened-in porch. Next to it is the cookhouse. And on the opposite side of the barn there is the tank house, the bottom floor of which would turn out to be my father's office. There is also a blacksmith shop, several storage sheds, and a long shelter to park tractors. Toward the periphery of the compound, almost swallowed up by the vineyards, are several other ramshackle homes with red sides and sagging roofs like ours for employees who qualify for company housing. About a quarter of a mile down a dirt road, I see more industrial-type buildings. These I learn later, are a dehydrator and a fruit drying shed.

They call it the "home ranch," and it turns out to be in excess of 2,000 acres—a substantial holding—90 per cent in grapes –pungent sweet dark varieties like Malagas, Zinfandels, and Muscatels that ferment into thick, sugary dessert wines and apple green Thompson seedless that sun-dry into sweet, sticky raisins. Almost as an afterthought, there are small acreages of apricots, peaches, nectarines, and alfalfa. About three-quarters of a mile west of the main compound is what they call "Camp Two," a long, low building with single rooms on each side and an acrid-smelling leaky common bathroom and laundry at its end. Camp Two is only used in the fall at picking time for migrant housing.

Constant use of caterpillar tractors on the farm's dirt roads has ground the soil into such fine silt that any vehicle traveling anywhere lifts up a cloud of dust. Fine particles of earth hover in the atmosphere and darken the sky most every day. Nothing moves without stirring up dust. It invades everything—the house, its rooms, closets, drawers, cupboards. Even things carefully wrapped and hidden away cannot escape the gritty, powdery film.

The owner and management, all the way down to the straw bosses are either first or second generation immigrants from Europe with one notable exception—Ira Cutler, the ranch foreman newly arrived from Texas. Behind his back, everybody calls him "Beech Nut" because that's the brand of tobacco he chews. In all the years I knew him, he was never without a telltale bulge between cheek and jaw and a tinge of brown oozing down the crease between the corner of his mouth and his chin. But the people who actually do the work here are almost exclusively Mexicans.

At a quarter to seven most every morning, Beech Nut ambles out to the barn and climbs up and sits on the top rung of the corral fence. He carefully loads up a wad of chew from the rectangular blue package it comes in. Slowly and deliberately folds the packet back to its original shape and slides it back into his blue work shirt pocket. Then he spits a couple of loose splashers in the direction of the mules who take little notice and proceeds to assign jobs for the day. And then at seven, the stable boy pulls the rope next to the tank house to activate the bell in its rafters, and the workmen begin to disappear into the ocean of grapevines and orchards—some to irrigate, some to drive tractors, some to "French" or "single" plow, some to harvest, tie, weed, load, unload, spray, or dust. The bell rings again at twelve and one, punctuating the lunch hour, and finally at five—quitting time.

Dad pays $7.50 for an ancient bicycle from a ranch hand so that I can pedal three miles down the narrow country road in front of the ranch to a tiny store run by some Japanese people and buy as many supplies as I can fit into my rucksack—cleanser and Brillo pads, a pound of ground meat, a cube of butter, a small bag of potatoes, a quart of milk, with a loaf of bread carefully balanced on top. The old man behind the counter uses an abacus to add up the bill.

About a month later, without telling anyone, Father gets a ride to Madera and buys a 1931 Chevrolet coupe with a rumble seat in the back for $85.00. Being as short as he is, he looks under the steering wheel to see where he is going. When making a turn, he never pulls the steering wheel around in a continuous arc, but pushes it up a small distance with one hand, holds it momentarily with the other, and frantically repeats the process over and over. On his way home, right at the entrance to the ranch by the palm trees, he misses the turn completely and drives point blank into a half-filled irrigation ditch. Both front wheels and the bottom of the motor compartment end up under water. The first person to come by is Mr. Alvira, the blacksmith, who laughs broadly but promises help.

Alvira and his son Gilbert start up the small John Deer tractor, the one they call "the jitterbug," and amid a lot of chuckling from a small crowd of ranch hands and children, we all head down to pull Dad out. They get a big kick out of 'helpin' the little guy out,' as Alvira puts it. It confirms their suspicions about city people—lots of book learning but little real know how. After it dries out, the car starts up without hesitation—only a couple of nicks here and there to remind us of the embarrassment.

Dad tells me Mr. Cutler says it's okay for me to get a job.

So at a quarter to seven the next morning, dressed in new Levi's and a work shirt, with my father's dollar watch in my pocket, I go out to the corral with the rest of them and wait my turn. Beech Nut puts me to picking apricots. And right away, Mike, my straw boss, a real sourpuss from the old country, starts yelling.

"Hey, boy! Hey, boy . . ." he strides over in a huff, hands flailing in the air, "You pickee too damn green, too damn green, boy! If you no see fruit is ripe—feel, feel. Take your finger like dis and feel. God damnee!"

They use ten-foot long, three-legged ladders to get the fruit down from the trees, and one time the back leg of my ladder sinks unexpectedly into some soft, wet dirt, and the whole thing tips over backwards with me on it. I wrench my wrist and scuff the palm of my hand trying to stop my fall and spill and bruise just about all the fruit in my bag. Thank God, Mike wasn't there to see it. As the afternoon heat begins to soar, the time drags and drags on interminably. I keep looking at Dad's watch every five minutes disappointed that so little time has passed. What a relief to see five o'clock finally roll around. And once home, I wash up, hurry through dinner and crash into bed.

The next day, Gilbert, the blacksmith's son, is also assigned to pick apricots, and so now at least there is someone to talk to. Gilbert is tall and lanky with a handsome profile, jet black hair, and glossy black eyes. He tells me about high school, how he is on the baseball team; he tells me about the ranch, about how to pick fruit, about the need to wear a broad-brimmed hat to ward off the sun, where to find cool water, and how to get along with Mike by always saying "Sure, Mike, sure."

Gilbert and his family turn out to be our neighbors since his father, as the blacksmith, qualifies for company housing. That night I walk over to their house and meet everybody, his mom, his dad and his younger brother Tony. Their place reminds me of a petting zoo—chickens, ducks, pigeons, a milk cow, two noisy peacocks, a huge garden, even a beehive. Gilbert's mother loads me down with two big bags of onions, tomatoes, cucumbers, squash and carrots.

When the apricots peter out, Beech Nut assigns me to help Gilbert's father in the blacksmith shop.

I love it. Mr. Alvira is a solid, thick-chested guy with steel-gray hair. When he's working, he always wears a greasy black skullcap and an equally spotted leather apron.

"Pancho," he calls me. "I can see your daddy is a pretty honest fella. At least now we know that if we work, we'll get what the hell is coming to us and no cabrón is gonna deduct a bunch of bullshit like extra meals we never ate. It's good to have an honest guy in that office for a change. You just lemme know if anybody gives him a hard time."

When I work in the blacksmith shop, the days pass like nothing ever. Mr. Alvira built his own hearth out of firebrick. It's my job to turn the rotary bellows and get the fire white hot. Then he positions the plowshares right into the hottest part of the coals, and in just a few minutes, the blades glow cherry red. He plucks them out deftly with metal tongues, lays them on the anvil, and pounds them to the desired shape and thickness with obvious strength and an artist's touch. While they are still blazing hot, he plunges them into a large barrel of black oil and they explode with a loud, steamy hiss. "That's the way you temper steel, hijo," he explains. After they cool, I get to sharpen them on a rotary power grinder wearing the goggles he gives me. Every once in a while, I notice him going into the storage shed and down something hidden in a crumpled brown paper bag—booze I figure. No question about it. By the end of the day, he's got a pretty good-sized buzz on. "They hate us, Pancho," he tells me, "the gabachos, the whities, the red necks like Beech Nut. They hate our guts because we're Mexicans. First they took our land and then our women . . . And all we do is bow and scrape . . . It's a fuckin shame Pancho."

My stint in the blacksmith shop lasts only a couple of days, and because the apricots are all finished, there is nothing for Gilbert and me to do but cut weeds—the worst job on the ranch—digging up Bermuda and Johnson grass. They call it 'workin' on the chain gang' especially if Mike is your straw boss. Both Bermuda and Johnson have long segmented roots botanists call rhizomes. Each little segment, if left in the soil, will start a whole new plant. Bermuda is low and thick with matted roots; Johnson gets to be five or six feet tall with long tough, fat, intertwined roots.

"Get root! Get root, boy, God dammee!" Mike yells as he stands there watching me try to dig out some stubborn roots with my shovel. By lunch time, I'm exhausted. We look for some shade under a vine. The Mexicans start a small fire from dead pieces of grapevine and roast tortillas on makeshift grills fashioned from loose vineyard wire. A bunch of them play craps until Mike makes us get back to work. With the temperature somewhere around 105, covered with dust and sweat, and pesky little bugs flitting into our faces, the going gets tough and tougher especially in the afternoon. It's great to hear relief coming as the truck comes plowing through the dust a few minutes before five.

Mike tells us that he has to go to town the following Friday afternoon to answer some questions about his income tax. That leaves ten of us all alone in the middle of this vast vineyard miles from anywhere—on our honor. Even before we see his black Plymouth coup disappear into the dust, someone has already taken up a collection and two of our guys hurry down to where one of the irrigators is working and gets him to drive them to the store for beer. They come back with two cases of Regal Pale in quart bottles. We cart the beer into the middle of a row so nobody can spot us, sit under some vines, and pass around bottle after bottle. I get the impression they all want Gilbert and me to get smashed—the elders initiating the young. And it isn't long before I become woozy, then dizzy and finally nauseous. They are singing the most beautiful songs I think I've ever heard—all in harmony—and every once in a while, one of them lets out a great cry—"un grito" they call it—a long piercing "Aaaa-aa-yy," like 'Here we are world! On the chain gang, in this boiling, blistering, fucking vineyard, but still full of manhood, full of dignity . . . full of orgullo—pride—' "AAAAYYEEEE!"

"Hey, Pancho, you don't look so good," Enrique teases. General laughter.

"If I look as bad as I feel," I confess, "I must look awful."

"Well," he says, "how would you like a special kinda cigarette?" He gives me a knowing wink. "Make you feel real good again, just like that—just 25 cents."

I give him the money but almost choke smoking it. It makes me so ill I crawl beneath a couple of vines into another row and retch until my sides ache. They help me both on and off the truck.

I expected my folks to really give me hell, but they think my being drunk is hilarious. I hadn't seen my mother laugh like that in years.

"Get the boy something to eat," Father shouts, "and some hot coffee."

"Der ist besoffen," she gloats, giggling.

And me? I just head for bed.

The next morning Father explains that Mike has claimed two exemptions on his income tax which of course is a lie. Everybody knows he's single. That's probably why the IRS wanted to talk to him he tells us. Not only that, but he marked himself down for nine hours on the time sheet for yesterday, even though we all know he was in Madera all afternoon. "Oh, but keep shush," he whispers sarcastically. "About the anointed we don't say a single word—nothing, right?—Sshhhh," he says as he puts his finger over his lips.

So then Mother gets a job cutting fruit in the drying shed. They set a 25lb. box of nectarines in front of her, and she has to cut each fruit in half, pit it, and place the two halves face up on a wooden tray. After she finishes the box, the "fruit boy" brings her another, while the checker, who just happens to be Beech Nut's wife, a matronly lady with curled white hair, comes over and punches her ticket with aloof reserve. Each punch is worth 12 cents.

Many a night, Father puts the front leg of his chair through the hole of a short piece of wood I fashioned for him. The metal peg of his cello bites into the board so that the instrument won't slip. Boccherini, Haydn, and Bach—his jaw juts back and forth as he bows with raw fury, the sweat pouring down his face onto his blue work shirt. And on Saturdays, Mother places her hearing aid right in front of the speaker of our tiny radio and listens to the Metropolitan Opera with Milton Cross all the way from New York. I can see her lips move with the text especially when they do German operas—even the Wagner.

"Why do you listen to that stupid Nazi crap?" I taunt.

"Babelee, babelee bab," she answers making a deprecating hand motion. "What do you know? Just a baby you are—still wet behind the ears. Ja. Babilee, babilee, bab—you chust shut up," she laughs.

And then one morning, Beech Nut puts me to cutting alfalfa—15 acres that grow in between rows of apricot trees. They irrigated the field after we finished picking, and by now the alfalfa is about 16 inches high. Attached to my small tractor is an eight foot scissors-blade that rides along the ground and whirrs back and forth cutting the alfalfa at its base, just like a barber cuts hair. I ride back and forth all day and by late afternoon just bounce along in a semi-stupor, bored and sluggish. A loud, blood-curdling scream explodes me out of my lethargy. I look down. A cat is caught in the blades. Shit! The animal's body is so intertwined in the cutting tines that they are totally stuck and will not move. I forget that the tractor is moving, though slowly and BAM my head blasts into an overhanging branch from an apricot tree. For a moment I feel like my head is the only thing that's keeping the tractor from moving forward as the cat squeals its last. Totally panicked, I punch in the clutch, shut the tractor off, and just sit there, shell-shocked. It's a struggle to extricate the cat. Luckily I find some running water in an adjacent vineyard and wash the blood off my hands from the cat and off my head from where I crashed into the tree—and continue on.

That Saturday night, Gilbert and me along with three other ranch hands each give a guy a dollar to drive us to Ryan's Arena in Fresno to see "La Lucha Libre," the wrestling matches. All six of us crowd into the tiny smoke filled auditorium crammed to the gills with noisy, raucous farm hands. Most of them have gotten off work at noon and have already been out shopping, eating and drinking. "Cervesa bien helada," cry the vendors. "Ice cold beer."

The plot is simple enough at the luchas—heroes fight villains—good versus evil. Mankind hopes for virtue but expects vice.

And the meanest villain ever to get into the ring is wrestling tonight. Ironically, he goes by the name of "Brother Love," a wily, brutish-looking hulk who masquerades as a pastor. Before he makes his entrance, the kid who works for him, dressed up as an altar boy, comes out and smokes up the aisles with incense. He sprinkles what is supposed to be holy water all around the ring. And finally Brother makes his entrance; he climbs in between the ropes wearing a frock and collar, kneels, crosses himself and offers up a prayer for victory. Then his opponent arrives—Luis Gomez—a clean-cut young Mexican wrestler, advertised as the "Pride of Jalisco." A guy next to the ring hits the bell with a hammer, bong, bong, and Brother starts right in by pulling Luis's hair, choking him and kneeing him in the groin. Then somehow he intertwines Luis's arms and legs into the ropes in such a manner that the poor guy can't get himself loose. As the referee is trying to free him, the altar boy hands Brother a burning cigarette which, after he shows it to the audience to make sure they know it's live, he repeatedly pokes and grinds into Luis's eyes while the referee's back just happens to be turned. The crowd roars in horror—Gilbert and me too. Even though we suspect that the whole thing is a big set-up, we scream and jeer just like everybody else.

Overcome by Brother's cruelty, an old woman on crutches, probably also a set-up, hobbles down to ringside. She lifts one of her crutches high in the air and commences swinging it as hard as she can trying to hit Brother. But he leans way out of the ring and with a diabolical leer anticipates her swing, intercepts the crutch and in a fit of rage breaks it into small pieces over the turnbuckle. As the crowd howls in anger, he hurls some of the pieces back at her grazing her head several times. Luis finally gets free from the ropes and goes into a wild dance of righteous indignation pounding his chest. Heck, even good guys get mad when they're pushed too hard. The crowd cheers him on wildly, and then, for a while fortunes shift in Luis's favor as he starts to beat up on Brother. That gets the crowd to cat-calling, taunting and hooting. Revenge, revenge, how sweet it is! Realizing his situation is worsening, Brother suddenly drops down to his knees and starts praying for mercy. He peers up at Luis from the canvas so totally humble, so innocent and holy—like a sweaty, muscle-bound angel, he pleads with his opponent not to beat up on him anymore. That confuses Luis who doesn't know what to do. How can you punish a man who is trying to make amends, who is praying to his Maker? But the crowd doesn't trust Brother and lets Luis know it. "Kill him," they yell. "Beat his fuckin' brains in," they scream. But Luis, always the gentleman, hesitates, walking around the ring puzzled and troubled. That's just the opening Brother needs because he crawls up behind his opponent, turns him around quickly and delivers such a smash to his groin that I can feel it 15 rows away from the ring. Luis doubles up. The referee gestures to Brother that it isn't very nice to hit your opponent like that, but Brother pays no attention. He grabs Luis by the hair and chokes him to near unconsciousness. Then lifts him up and gives him his specialty— the spectacular, unstoppable helicopter death spin. After a half-dozen gyrations, Brother drops his by now totally dazed opponent onto the canvas like a limp sack, then dives on him pinning him to the count of three. He jumps up victoriously and parades around the ring like a rooster. Then, with the crowd still booing fiercely, he kneels down to pray. Evil in the guise of good has triumphed. The altar boy helps him on with his cleric's frock and precedes him up the aisle, once again dispensing copious amounts of incense and holy water.

The two wrestlers in the final match try their best to get something started, but there is no more emotion left. Brother Love and the good guy from Jalisco have purged it all. It will make a great story to tell everyone and pass the time out there in the field.

*

When September rolls around, four of us—Gilbert, his little

brother Tony, Ismelda, the daughter of the couple who run the cookhouse, and I walk down in the cool mornings along the palm trees to where the dirt intersects the paved road and wait for the school bus. I can't believe school. Compared to Brooklyn, there are hardly any students. Where we had 60 and 70 in algebra, Spanish and English back east; out here, there aren't even 20. All our Spanish teacher does is play records, show movies and talk about Mexican food. School is a continuous round of assemblies, sports, dances, plays, and programs.

And then, in just the second week of the semester, one morning on our way to school, our bus is flat-out run into by a drunk driver who, we hear later, was already totally tanked at eight o'clock in the morning. The guy runs a stop sign and hits us so hard that we tip over into a dry ditch underneath a guidewire next to a power pole. About an hour later, another school bus comes along to pick us up, and we all feel like great heroes walking around school with notes pinned to the front of us saying that because of the "ordeal" we had just been through, we were excused from classes till after lunch.

Gilbert and I have two classes together—algebra and physics—and we often study together. It's a rationalization I know, but I often think that if it hadn't been for physics, I wouldn't have done one of the stupidest things I've ever done in my whole life. My folks had bought an ancient refrigerator whose top mounted compressor looked like a stack of white dishes. It sat on the porch clickity clacking away continuously—day and night—seemingly never shutting off, and yet the inside of the refrigerator was as warm—maybe warmer—than the outside. I decided it was probably out of coolant and because our physics book said that ammonia is used as a coolant, Gilbert and me put some in. We carefully loosened the copper tubing next to the freezer compartment and delicately funneled in about a cup and a half of household ammonia. After sealing everything back up, we started her up, and I stayed out there hour after hour, my hand on the shelf of the freezer compartment hoping for the tiniest tingle of cool. But nothing. A couple of weeks later when the refrigeration man came and learned what I had done, he refused to add freon because he said the mixture would make hydrochloric acid and melt the whole thing into porridge. I argued with him, even showed him our physics textbook, but all he said is, yes, they do use ammonia in large cooling plants but not little boxes like ours. So our refrig was toast, and we had to resort to an old top-loading Coca Cola ice chest and start hauling blocks of ice and clean out the melt just like we did years ago in Brooklyn. My folks were easy on me because they knew I was just trying to help. It wasn't until a year later that we could afford another used refrigerator.

Then Gilbert's aunt got hit in the back with the corner of a wooden pick box as she was picking grapes. The way it happened is that a couple of braceros were distributing empty wooden pick boxes off a mule-drawn vineyard wagon supposedly ahead of the pickers. Why she was picking where they were throwing empties, or conversely, why they were throwing boxes where people were picking remains a mystery. Not that anyone thinks they did it on purpose. They just didn't see her under a vine and the corner of that wooden crate smashed right into her spine like a spear. I made a big fuss about it to my father, but because, in those days, farm workers weren't insured, there was no going to the doctor. She ended up being treated by a curandero, a shaman, and never again in her whole life walked right. Gilbert's father took it hard.

*

Reading the paper, my mother notices that the movie *Die Fledermaus* (*The Bat*), the world famous musical comedy by the waltz king Johann Strauss is playing at the White Theater in Fresno. As usual father doesn't want to go, so I take her. She holds on to my arm real tight as we amble over from where we parked the car and head into the movie house. The film is in German with English subtitles—in a practically deserted theater. It's all about masked balls with women in splendid gowns and men in military dress uniforms frenziedly waltzing across the screen—lot of mistaken identities, stage drunks and pratfalls. She loves every moment of it, and to my amazement, knows the score perfectly, even starts singing the words out loud along with the actors.

After the movie, I take her to an all-night diner just off the highway, and she leans across the table, "When your mother was girl, Franz," she says, "you know, we used to be so lustig . . . so merry, so cheerful, so happy—not a care in the world—sing and dance and go to parties . . . And listen, it's not like there weren't others . . . not like I didn't have chances . . . ah, many . . . but that man never needs nothing, not a damned thing He could live out there in that desert all by himself . . . Just like tonight, he never wants to go nowhere . . . Just plays his verdamnte cello to the grapepickers . . . And they don't care—don't care a bit . . . How crazy. So what is there to do? The man is dotti, you know . . . dotti . . . but he's all I got."

Meanwhile, the waitress has come over and wants our order. "What's it gonna be, folks?"

My mother studies her for a moment. "Do you serve French cuisine?" she asks, knowing of course, that she's never been in a local restaurant that does.

"What? What does she want?" the waitress asks me in a quandary.

"Never mind," I tell her. "Just give us two hamburgers and two cups of tea."

*

That Saturday afternoon, Gilbert and me climb the storm fence around the irrigation pond by the big pump near the apricot orchard and swim in three-foot deep water. Though chilly, the water is clear and sweet, and after splashing back and forth a few times, we settle on top of the earthen berm around the pond, drying out in the soft sun and start smoking Chesterfields.

"After high school," I tell him, "I think I'll work out here for a year, save my money, and go to the college down in Fresno."

"Unless I get a baseball scholarship, I won't be joining you, Pancho."

"Why not? Heck, you should go, Gilbert," I tell him. "You get good grades."

"Ah, I'm just a Mexican. Mexicans aren't supposed to go to college. We're just good for the field," he laughs.

"Bullshit," I say. "You do good in algebra and physics."

"Nah," he tells me, "if I went to college, Mike and Beech Nut would miss me."

Just then one of the week-end irrigators wearing knee-high black rubber boots, shovel over shoulder, appears from out of the orchard. "Hey," he hollers much agitated, "you guys not suppose to be in dere. Peligroso! Danger! Big fuckin' danger—220 volt on that chingada pump! You guys all wet—aye, Dios mio!—knock you locitos clear to Chihuahua!"

So we climb out and calm him down and offer him a Chesterfield. He sits on his haunches leaning on his shovel, inhales deeply and thoughtfully, savoring the moment.

"Hey," he says, "they's a bunch a women over there at Camp Two, hijos," he winks. "Si-mon, hijos, cinco dollares, muchachos . . . Fi dolla, Pancho."

We look at each other.

"I don't have no money on me," Gilbert says.

"Me neither."

"But we know where we can get some . . . right?" he laughs, "at home . . . Right, Pancho? Come on."

"Well, I don't know . . ."

"You chicken, huh? Come on. Let's get us some a those chulas. Come on. There sure as hell ain't nothing better to do around here."

"Well, all right," I agree hesitatingly, and we hustle home.

The mules are standing still in the corral. It's Saturday afternoon, and they too get the afternoon off. They huddle together in clumps of five and six, head to rear—tails swishing rhythmically to keep the flies off their brothers and sisters. They turn and watch us vacantly, and then one starts to urinate. That sets them all off—twenty or more, all in unison—a strange intrusion into the calm of a Saturday afternoon, like a waterfall on a rock.

The door to my father's office is open which means he's in there working on the payroll. As I step inside the screen door of the porch of our house, I can hear the opera. I peek into the kitchen; she's knitting, transfixed, with her hearing aid in front of the radio—*Boris Godunov*. That makes it easy to sneak into my room and lift a soft green fiver out of the little bank on the dresser and a couple of condoms hidden in between some books on the shelf. As I stick them into my pocket, I remember how embarrassed I was when the school nurse talked to us about "protection" in biology class.

Avoiding the main roads, we make our way to Camp Two through parallel rows out in the vineyard. It takes about twenty minutes. A ranch hand motions us to one of the last doors with a shrug. The room is divided horizontally and vertically with olive drab army blankets hanging on clotheslines. Another blanket is tacked over the single window so that the only light comes from a solitary bulb hanging by a wire from the ceiling. An old lady, very friendly, meets us at the door; she collects our money and tells us to sit down. It is then that I realize that at that very moment there is activity in the room. Right there behind those blankets just a few feet from where we're sitting are some guys having sex with a bunch of prostitutes. Wow! Just then a tall, middle-aged woman with jet black hair comes out from behind one of the blankets and the old woman says, "Well, hijos, who wants her?"

"Go ahead, Pancho," Gilbert tells me, and I duck in behind one of the blankets with her. She immediately drops her shift and steps out of it totally naked—boom—just like that. Then lies down on the cot, one leg outstretched, the other dangling. I notice some nasty black and blue marks up over her breast on one side and ask, "What happened there?" but she just reaches up towards me and pulls down my pants.

Matter-of-factly she peels off the squishy condom, flings it in the trashcan, squats down on the floor and commences to clean herself with a washcloth that has been soaking in a sudsy basin.

*

Neither of us speaks for some time.

"Gimme a cigarette, Gilbert," I ask. "I'm out."

"Hey, man, when you gonna buy your own?" he says half annoyed. "Here, you little shit," he pulls out a pack, takes one, and give me one, and we light up.

"How was yours?" I ask.

"Cherry, man." God, everything seems to be "cherry" with Gilbert lately.

"And you? The big brunette, huh?" he laughs.

"Yeah, and I did it two times," I lied.

"Ah, you're full of it," he says. "Whores don't let you come twice—not good for business."

We're still walking through the vineyard, through a patch of Malagas that hadn't been picked yet, and I reach over, pull off a bunch, blow the dust off, eat a couple, and give him a cluster.

"How many times do you suppose they do it?" I ask.

"All day and all night. As long as there are horny guys like you and me out there," he answers. "If you went back there right now, they wouldn't even recognize you."

"Wow, they must get worn out."

"Nah, you can't wear out sex. It's made that way."

When we get back to the bunkhouse, a bunch of guys are standing around Albert Garcia, the tractor driver. Even on a Saturday afternoon, he's been out there disking and now is completely covered with dust, like a coal miner with goggles up on his forehead. He is petting a black widow spider. The thing is crawling over his bare hand—a live, fat, black patent leather marble-like body whose bite can kill you, with long slithery legs and a fiery red spot in the middle of her belly.

"As long as you pet her, and love her, nothing happens. You see that?" he says as he strokes the spider with his free hand. "Just like a beautiful woman," he continues. "You have to cuddle and stroke her . . . Don't just go in there in between her legs like an animal," he makes a humping motion, "cause she don't like that. That's when she'll bite you." By now the spider is crawling on his grimy leather jacket, leaving a trail in the dust.

I walk over to our house and take a cold bath.

At five o'clock Father gets home and tells us that the sheriff is out at Camp Two picking up a bunch of prostitutes.

"Oh, my God," says Mother. "Trash trash! Gutter trash! That's all there is around here," she shakes her hands emphatically.

"Why do we have to live here? Such a hell hole I tell you. And this heat! I come through the Nazis, and New York, but I tell you this is the worst hell hole on the face of the earth—schrecklish! The lowest scum, bah!"

"Not again," he exclaims looking at me. "See what I have to put up with?" He takes a couple of steps toward her. "Where else can we go?" he shouts. "Not a young man I am any more, you understand. Very limited our choices here. I mean everything is quite satisfactory, isn't it?"

"Don't shout so," she yells back at him, then turns and flees into their bedroom, slamming the door.

*

The rains came early this year—about a week before the end of September. Big, big trouble for the raisins. They're still out there in the damp, drippy vineyard lying on mushy paper trays. If the weather continues wet, thousands and thousands of tons of half-dried grapes will mildew and rot—an immense loss. It is precisely for this reason that the company has built a dehydrator. Not only can they save their own crops, they can charge other farmers to save theirs. Dad tells me they're gonna need plenty of help to work evenings and weekends—time and a half. So Gilbert and me sign up right away. The technology is simple enough; just roll a long line of narrow gauge carts loaded with half-dried raisins into long concrete tunnels. Shut the doors and start blowing hot air through the tunnels. In twelve hours—raisins.

The following Saturday, at seven in the morning we start unwrapping rolled brown paper trays and spreading half-dried mushy grapes onto weather beaten wooden trays. We face the trays the long way on the carts so that the air can blow through them, stack them over six feet high and roll the loaded carts into the tunnels. By half-past seven in the evening, we have all twelve long tunnels crammed to the gills with tons and tons of produce. The large counter-weighed doors are sealed and locked, the heating oil is ignited, and the blowers commence roaring away. Time to clean up—which means push brooms, steam and water hoses, and snow shovels to clean layers and layers of raisin muck off the concrete deck. It's already after eight and tonight our straw boss also wants us to clean the big shunting turntable—the one they use to steer the carts into the desired tunnel. We start by lifting up the heavy wooden planks on top of the eight foot circular steel frame. And then with three standing in the well, and three on the lip, we lift the massive steel wheel from the center post, out of the concrete race at its circumference. Gingerly we tilt the monster up on end and carefully roll it up against one of the tunnel walls. Then with the aid of a steam hose, we clean out enough raisin gunk to fill a large steel drum.

"Horale, muchachos," says one, "let's get this son of a biscuit back in there." So we carefully roll it back next to the well.

"Okay, we'll lift it from the outside," says another. "Gilbert, you grab the plate on the inside in the center, right by the hole and guide it onto the post."

"Aayy," says a third. "He could find it better if you put a little hair around it." Laughter.

But as soon as we start tipping it, the massive steel wheel starts to slip on the wet concrete.

"Stop it. Stop it!" I shout. "Watch out! Gilbert, watch out! The fuckin' thing is coming down on you. Gilbert! It's falling too fast. Watch it!"

We strain and struggle and desperately fight to stop it from falling, to hold it up, to keep it from slipping on the wet concrete, but somehow we're off balance; it's too heavy and has too much momentum and just keeps angling down. And then, with no warning, just a raspy screech it crashes down and slams right in place on the center post—BAM!—with Gilbert's hand right in there!

"My God!" I shout.

"It's bit my hand!" he screams. "Aye, Dios mio! My fingers! My hand! It lopped off my hand!"

I jump over and grab him by the shoulders. "Gilbert! Gilbert!" God! His hand is a bloody mess.

"Look at his hand," says one.

"His hand," says another.

It looks like parts of a couple fingers are missing—deep crimson pieces of flesh hanging down and blood pouring out over everything. Everything is happening so fast. Now what are we gonna do? Somebody yanks the first aid kit off the wall and hands it to me. In confusion I pull apart a large package of gauze dressing and wrap it over and around his hand hoping it would hide the wound—erase the damage. But although the bandage turned bright red, it did seem to stop the bleeding. And then it comes to me that my father told me that there was insurance for people working in the dehydrator—They're "industry," he told me, not "farm." So I run over to the office and tell the boss. He comes over with a big flashlight and tells me to take Gilbert to his parents' house and have them take him to the hospital in Madera right away.

"My parents aren't home," Gilbert blurts out. "My parents aren't home . . . They went to Stockton to visit my aunt and uncle."

"I'll take him," I tell him.

"Wait a minute. Lemme get the insurance form from the office," he says and runs off.

And returns in just a couple of minutes. "Here, go see Cutler," he tells me, "and tell him I said you should take the company pickup."

By this time, one of the guys has made a sling for Gilbert's arm out of a big blue handkerchief, and the two of us walk over to Beech Nut's house in the dark. I jog up through the yard, up on his porch and knock on the front door as Gilbert waits in the shadows.

"We had a bad accident over in the dehydrator, Mr. Cutler," I explain. The boss over there sent me here. Gilbert lost a couple of fingers. He told me to take him to Madera in the company pickup."

He looks at me in silence and frowns. "Shit!" he says. "Stupid Mexicans!" He leans out the front door and spits past me. "Yeah, all right." He thrusts his hand into his overall pocket and fishes out the keys to the pickup. "Go ahead and take him," he says. "It needs gas," he goes on. "Go over to the gas tank and fill her up; this is the key to the pump."

We get in the pickup which is parked just a few feet away and drive away in silence. I'm just concentrating on keeping the pickup on my side of the yellow divider. Orchards, vineyards, pastures, road-signs, fences, gates, mailboxes, farmhouses, the lights from on-coming cars fly by like in a dream.

And then, about half way to town, Gilbert turns to me. "Pancho," he says, "the parts that got chopped off . . . They're probably lying out there some place . . . Pancho, do me a favor? Un favor? Let's go back and see if we can find them in the well. Maybe they can sew them back on, okay? If I don't do it now, I'll lose my fingers, Pancho, for the rest of my life. Pancho, please?"

I'm thinking this has to be the craziest idea ever, but I don't say nothing. I don't believe anything is lying in that well back there, nothing but some ground-up strips of tissue, maybe a sliver or two of bone or nail, but I can't tell him that. A guy has the right to look for his own damned fingers, don't he?

So I tell him "Okay," and make a U-turn, and we drive back. When we get there, he just stands there as all of us once again take the planks out and lift the stupid turntable out of the well. The boss shines his flashlight all around, but there is nothing to see, nothing to find—just a couple of dark brown stains mixed with lubricating oil on the center post. Head down, he walks back out to the pickup, and we start out again.

When we finally make it to the hospital, it's after ten already. It really isn't a hospital—just a kind of emergency room in a clinic. The doctor on duty is at the movies across the street. So the nurse and I hustle over to fetch him. The projectionist puts a small yellow insert in one corner of the screen. "Dr. Reynolds, please report out front."

He looks at Gilbert's hand and tells us that both fingers will have to be trimmed down to the next joint. All in all, he will lose two joints on his index finger and one on the middle finger of his right hand.

When Gilbert hears this, he goes frantic. "Pancho, Pancho," he cries, "I cut off half of my damned fingers, and now this pinchi cabrón wants to cut off the rest. Don't let him do it. Pancho, Pancho, I need your help. Please."

"You broke off the bone in an uneven way, young man,"

the doctor tells him. "that makes the ends very sharp and splintery. If we don't trim them, you'll be in pain every time you use those fingers. They'll never heal," he says. "Sorry, but we have to take them down to the next joint." And after anesthetizing the hand, that's exactly what he does.

By the time we leave the clinic, it's almost twelve.

"What a night!" Gilbert says as we amble back to the pickup, his hand all wrapped in white gauze as fat as a beehive. "And my folks aren't even home. God! What are they gonna say?"

"Maybe we should call 'em as soon as we get home."

"And it's my right hand," he says accusingly, "my throwing hand. There goes the fuckin' scholarship."

"Gilbert, you never know."

"Pancho, will you quit shittin' me . . . Let's go get a couple of beers. One beer for each finger."

"Gilbert, no. Shit man, it's too late. You've been working since seven this morning. You've been through too much. You gotta get some rest. And we gotta call your folks."

"Oh, screw that," he says annoyed.

"Besides, they won't sell us no beer."

"Bullshit, you just don't want to go, do you? Hey look, I heard everything. I heard Beech Nut call me a dumb Mexican. And you probably agree with him. So go ahead to your fuckin' college. I got no reason . . ."

"All right! All right! We'll go then," I tell him.

It only takes a few minutes to find a cantina. We push through the swinging doors into the cigarette haze, into the thumping two-step ranchera music. There are lots of people in there just like every Saturday night—drinking at tiny round tables, a few dancing on the small dance floor with a three-piece band up front. Once people find out what happened to Gilbert, they buy us beer galore. There is no stopping them. In just ten minutes, our whole table is full of bottles and cans of beer and Gilbert is getting wild. He starts singing Mexican songs along with the band and giving gritos while everybody cheers.

"Pancho," he points to the far end of the room. "You see

that chula over there?"

"Oh, shit, Gilbert! Not that!"

"Screw you, Pancho," he looks at me in anger. "Me, I'm gonna dance with that chula over there. You just fuckin' watch me." But as soon as he stands up, he starts to rock back and forth and keels over. A couple of guys help me get him into the pickup, and it's not till after two before I get him to bed. I park the pickup where I found it; leave the keys in it, and walk home.

*

Gilbert didn't go to school the next Monday or the next week, not even the next month. The first time I saw him again was a couple of months later as he waved to me from his new motorcycle with Ismelda clutching him tight from behind. I don't remember either one of them ever going back to school, and I guess nobody down at that high school was ever all that concerned about two Mexican kids from way out in the country missing school. A few weeks later, Tony told me that Ismelda and his brother had moved to the foothills where he's working on an orange ranch.

*

That December, Pearl Harbor starts WW II. My brother Fritz calls us from New York and tells us he's joined the Army. Our school bus never again picks up any of the Japanese kids on our route. There's a rumor on the bus that the owners of the little grocery store where we do our shopping have a machine gun hidden in the wood pile behind the store and talk to the Emperor every night over their short wave radio. I don't believe any of that for a minute. Soon all the Japanese around Madera have to sell or rent their farms, houses, cars—everything—usually for practically nothing. They're all to be interned into camps inland. But first they're rounded up and detained at the Madera County Fairgrounds which now has barbed wire and sentry towers all around it. The same place where Gilbert and I went to see the burlesque show last summer at the fair, where we paid an extra quarter a piece at the end of the regular performance to stay to see a woman take off her clothes and pretend to make love to a lamppost.

*

And now, after all these years—after finishing college and getting a teaching job, and then getting drafted during the Korean War and stationed in Germany for 16 months, I was able to come back home and start teaching again. Meanwhile the ranch got sold, and the new owners fired everyone including Dad.

Of course, I've been wondering whatever happened to Gilbert. Dad told me his folks left the ranch a couple of years earlier probably while I was overseas. So I'm curious if I'll ever see Gilbert or Ismelda again. Hope they're still together and happy, living up there in the foothills among some lovely citrus groves.

*

The Marimba Band

fiction

At exactly two o'clock, Mrs. Thomas, the President's secretary, called. "It's the cover sheet, Dean," she insisted. "You're missing a signature on the cover sheet for that course you're tryin' to get through cabinet this afternoon."

"Oh, you mean the marimba class?" I asked.

"Yeah, I guess it's something like that," she sighed. "Just a minute . . . I need to check the stack right here."

"Well, I can't understand how we could be missing a signature. Seems like we got more people to sign-off on that thing than are needed for an initiative referendum."

"Ah, here it is," she interrupted. "Ethnic Studies 37, Marimba Band . . . You need the instructor's signature."

"The instructor's signature?" I winced. "Good heavens . . . What in the hell for?"

"Because the President said so, that's what in the hell for," she snapped.

"But we've never had to do that before. I mean, is this something new? After all, the President's cabinet's function here is to allow the class into the curriculum, not to schedule it. Not that our choice of instructor is such a big secret. Everybody knows it's gonna be Ralph Mendoza from the math department. If we get it through, he'll be teaching the class as an overload, just to get the kids started . . ."

"Look, Dean, I'm not here to argue with you about any of this stuff you're tellin' me," she cut in. "I don't have nothin' to do with all that. All I know is that the President told me that if the cover sheet for that class don't have the instructor's signature on it by three this afternoon, to just leave it in the office. It will not make it to cabinet today. Now if that's what you want, well, that's okay with me."

"All right. All right. You win," I conceded. "I'll be over in a few minutes to pick it up and see if I can find Ralph."

"Well, okay then. Good luck."

"Yeah."

Damn, I thought as I slammed the receiver down, put my coat on and hurried out through the outer office. "They're doin' it to us again," I blurted out to Mrs. Fernandez, our secretary, in passing.

*

After retrieving the cover sheet from Mrs. Thomas, I flew across the lawn by the water fountain, past the foyer to the theater and into the music building hoping to find Ralph. It was that time in the afternoon when music from quite a few divergent musical groups blend into a strange cacophony of sound through the mostly deserted hallways—woodwinds from one room, jazz from another, the marching band from down the hall, a barbershop quartet pining for the good old days—and, ah, I recognized the strong bass line of the marimba band. I was in luck. They were practicing today.

Ralph smiled when he saw me enter the back of the room. I stayed by the door until the students finished the final chorus of an old favorite, "La Feria de las Flores" ("The Flower Fair"). Except for the shiny, brand new marimba up in front—the same marimba which had recently been donated by the owner of the Mexican movie house in town—the room came off dowdy and close, crowded with students, their instruments, music stands, sheet music, stacks of textbooks, sweaters, jackets and random chairs.

"Señor Dean, mucho placer a verle—good to see you, amigo." Ralph stepped out from behind the music stand from which he had been directing and put his hand on my shoulder. "Hey, amigo, did I ever tell you my parents and even one of my grandparents were born in this town? That means we've probably been livin' here longer than most a' you gringos." General laughter.

"Hi, Dean." it was Mrs. Fernandez's daughter Lydia in the front row with violin.

"Señor Dean, why such a sad face? Aye Dios mio," Ralph put in. "Hey, muchachos, maybe we need to cheer up this hombre here. Maybe we need to play him a nice ranchera. Maybe he needs a nice love song from the heart with spirit and soul—or something on the new marimba—Aye, la marimba, como cimbra!"

"Ralph—I mean Rafael—listen. There isn't time for all that. Listen, I gotta get you to sign this cockamamie curriculum proposal and shoot it right back to the President's office. Without it, there will be no Ethnic Studies 37, no Marimba Band, no nada. Comprende? Listen—Ralph—without it we won't even get the one lousy unit we settled for.

"All in good time, señor," he said. "But first let me show you where we think we can store the instruments." He pulled me through the clutter and into an adjoining walk-in closet which used to serve as a practice room before the new music addition came along.

"Voilà, señor. Look, there is plenty of room in here. We can roll the marimba over there by the window . . . and the cimbales over here, the guitars, violins, trompetas and saxophones all up on those shelves, qué no?"

Meanwhile the students started playing another song in the other room all on their own. Ralph looked pleased. "They're good kids, Dean," he beamed. "All excited about putting on a program for Cinco de Mayo."

"Well, they wouldn't be doing so well if they didn't have a good man like you to help them . . . Okay, this looks good, Ralph. Nobody I know of is using this old closet. It should work out fine."

"So, could we get the key?"

"I don't see why not. Give me a chance to talk to the music people. After the meeting the other day, you realize of course, they're a little tender."

I knew they would object because having the key to something defines it as your turf. Getting the key is going to require a confrontation—Well, hell, that's what they pay me for.

"Yes, I know," he said. "But we don't bother them."

"I understand. I know—So don't worry. I'll work something out. Give me a few days."

"Bueno. I'll leave it in your hands."

"Okay. But now, Ralph, I've got to get my butt over there to the President's office with that cover sheet. Come on. You've got to sign the damned thing." So now it was my turn to pull him back into the other room, and we walked over to the marimba.

"Okay," I said. "So where is it? I thought I left it right here." He looked confused.

"Where is what?"

"The form—the cover sheet—you know the paper with all those signatures on it." I started searching myself. "Hey, I know I walked in here with that damned paper . . . Ralph, I showed you that form, right?"

"Yeah, I remember you had something in your hand . . . Well it's got to be around here some place."

"I thought I put it right here on the edge of the marimba. It's kinda yellow—sort of a mustard color." I searched all around the marimba again, in and over the sound box. Nothing.

Then, just as I happened to look up I spied something yellow sticking out from underneath the mouthpiece of a saxophone a student was playing. I dashed over. The student stopped and produced half of the missing cover sheet from behind some arrangements. "Oh, is this what you were you looking for?" he asked with a grin. "I used half of it to wrap around the stem here so it wouldn't leak so much air." He took off the mouthpiece and started to unravel the missing other half.

"This sax is kinda beat up, and the mouthpiece leaks a lot of air. It helps if you wrap it."

I must have really stared at him because he said, "I'm sorry. I didn't know your paper was so important."

"I understand," I nodded, then looked at my wristwatch. My God, it was a quarter of three. I had exactly 15 minutes—hardly enough time to redo the damned thing. So I laid both halves of the cover sheet on the marimba and flattened them out as best I could.

"Here, Ralph. Here, sign it," I told him. "Somebody get me some Scotch tape." And luckily they found some in the teacher's desk.

By this time everyone had quit playing. They were all hovering around the marimba watching Ralph and me trying to smooth out the wrinkles, dry off the saliva, and tape the two halves together.

"It's a disaster, Ralph—Shit! This side is barely legible. But there just isn't time to do anything else. Hell, it'll just have to do—Wish me luck," I said and I was out the door walking as fast as I could back to the Administration Building.

*

I got to Mrs. Thomas just as she was emerging from the President's office on her way to cabinet. When she saw the condition of the cover sheet, she started to laugh. "My God, whatchoo do, shoot it?"

"I can explain . . ."

She used a little pull cart like the kind you see passengers use in airports to haul what appeared to be an almost three-foot high stack of handouts over to the conference room—reports, class outlines, recommendations, studies, agendas.

"Talk about paper shufflers," I laughed. "If the taxpayers only knew. Here, lemme pull that thing for you."

*

That day, the agenda was punishing—23 items—of which the absolute last one was "Approval of eight new curriculum offerings." I kept a pretty low profile during most of the afternoon except for the one time when I got into it with the Dr. Lynch, our Vice President. Lynch was advocating a new position for the college—"Director of Marketing." Good heavens! Positions like that are for the likes of big business and Wall Street banks, not for institutions of higher learning. "Why not put our money into hiring some more instructors?" I asked him. "We're already bustin' at the seams with P.R. people." No action was taken.

At about 5:30, the Director of Maintenance and the Coordinator of the Media Center ducked out. I knew exactly where they were headed—up to Henry's Cantina on Broad Street to down a couple before dinner. Fifteen minutes later Campus Police Chief Riley left, probably to join them. Good. I was glad to see all three of 'em leave because in all likilihood, they would vote against the marimba.

It wasn't until well after six that the cabinet took up the new curriculum offerings, which in alphabetical order were: Air Conditioning, a new class; Computer Science, five new classes; Dental Hygiene, one class revised; and Ethnic Studies, the Marimba Band, a new class. The first seven passed routinely. It didn't take more than a couple of minutes. And that's when the President noticed the screwed up cover sheet for the Marimba class. Though he looked shocked and irritated at first, I was relieved when, judging by his facial expression, he seemed to ease into curiosity and amusement. After a pause, he picked up the cover sheet by its very corner like a soiled napkin and held it high in the air. Time for late afternoon humor. "Well, Dean," he said, looking right at me, "from what dumpster did you extricate this course outline?" Much laughter, with particularly raucous guffaws from Dr. Lynch, who as always sat right next to the President, at the right hand of god.

"It's a long story . . . I'm embarrassed about it . . ." I half stammered. "And I apologize for the condition of that cover sheet." My ears were thumping. "There simply wasn't time to prepare a new one. But I promise I will do so first thing in the morning."

"You mean, provided it passes," added Lynch forcing another belly laugh.

"Yes, of course."

Vice President Lynch was enjoying himself. He leaned back expansively in his swivel chair. "Well," he said taking the cover sheet from the President. "Don't you think we ought to make it a rule that any course outline that comes in looking like this," he held it up high again, "like something the cat threw up on . . . ought not to be considered at all?" More laughter. Though I guessed Lynch was only trying to be funny, I half expected somebody to take him seriously. But nobody said anything.

"Well, let's get to it. It's already late enough," said the President. "Ladies and gentlemen, we're now considering Ethnic Studies 37, Marimba Band, one unit, four hours." He passed out copies of the course outline.

The Dean of Men, sitting very erect, arms folded across his

chest was first to speak. "I notice that this course doesn't call for a textbook. Isn't that rather unusual?" He looked around for support.

"Well," I explained, "the instructor is going to be doing different numbers and will be ordering appropriate musical arrangements. As many of you know, he is a full time math instructor here at the college and has played professionally for a number of years. I might just mention in passing that the music department has a number of similar ensembles of this type—strings, woodwinds, jazz, guitar, madrigals, and a barber shop quartet class. None of those classes require textbooks. They either rent, buy, or copy suitable music."

"Well, I suppose you know best," he answered grudgingly, "but I still think every college course ought to require the students to have a college-level textbook, not just a bunch of song sheets."

At which point, the Dean of the Business Division leaned halfway across the table and pointed himself at me. "Now have you worked out your articulation agreement with the university on this class? You know," he turned to everyone, "I don't think it's fair to our students to let them accrue a lot of these 'fun-type' units at our level just for singin' and playin' around a little . . . because, you see, once they get out there to that university, the units earned here may not be accepted, and unfortunately that's where our students lose out . . . That's where the real tragedy comes in, don't you see?"

"Most four-year institutions do allow units for participation in musical groups," I replied, trying my best to be patient. "Frankly, I believe our students will retain these credits. Of course, you can't guarantee that ahead of time. Once the course is in the curriculum, the four-year schools will look at it and decide whether or not to honor the units. But based on past experience, I'm almost certain they will. By the way, I have to take exception to the phrase 'a lot of units.' Even if students were to take this class for two years, that's every single semester they're going to school here, they would only come away with grand total of four units. And another thing, they don't just 'play around' in this class any more than they do in other ensemble classes. They have to be able to play instruments in the first place, read music and . . ."

"Let me leap in here," interrupted the President. "Are there any music faculty here to speak to this?"

Music faculty? Man, I hadn't expected that. Individual instructors never come to cabinet to debate specific classes. They do their thing at the Curriculum Committee level. . . This thing is wired!

"Yes," said Mrs. Bailey, our piano teacher. When had she come in I wondered?

"Well, we don't really have anything against it, I suppose," she said gingerly. "Except that some music instructors have told me they're a little uneasy about having someone teaching what is basically a music class who doesn't have a degree in music."

"That's right, he doesn't." I was really getting annoyed and stood up. "Ralph Mendoza, as I've already told you is a tenured mathematics instructor here at this college. He plays professionally in a salsa band on weekends and is eminently qualified to teach this class. As a matter of fact, the students have already been getting together all by themselves on a strictly *ad hoc* basis a couple of times a week. Incidentally, the cabinet should know that the music department currently has several non-music majors teaching part-time. One in fact is a stockbroker who plays second violin in our philharmonic and has taught music appreciation for us for years. Another is our guitar teacher who I don't think ever even finished high school."

"That's all well and good," interjected Dr. Lynch, who whenever he was trying to be serious had the curious ability to raise his eyebrows in such a way as to construct the top two sides of an almost perfect isosceles triangle, "but what about some of the budgetary implications? Are our taxpayers going to want to foot the bill for the expenses of just this one group—even though we're operating on a broad tax base? What I'm saying here is that the money that supports this one class seems to be coming from everybody, but benefits only this one group."

"Am I hearing this correctly?" I replied, really steamed. "Just a few minutes ago you people approved seven new courses almost all of which—especially the computer classes—called for tens and tens of thousands of dollars in capital expenditures—computers, room modifications, software, hardware—God knows what else—without so much as batting an eyelash. And now, all of a sudden, here comes this puny little one-unit Chicano class—this terrible threat—and you bring up all this petty garbage. In the first place, Dr. Lynch, all their instruments, including a $2,500 marimba have been donated, so that the college isn't out a single dime. And, as you all know, by state formula, we'll get more in attendance reimbursements to pay for the instructor's salary and the use of the room than it actually will cost us. So, you'll make money on the deal. Let me repeat that—Moneywise this school will come out way ahead.

"And furthermore, Dr. Lynch, this class in not limited to Chicano students. Anyone can attend." I knew I was losing it, but the more I thought about what was happening here, the madder I got. "Please understand," I said, "this kind of music is very popular with one out of four people in our community. It's popular throughout the whole country, even in the world—hundreds and hundreds of millions of people . . . And while I'm at it, let me just get something off my chest—It's quite obvious that if this were not a class requested by our Chicano students, it would have passed a long time ago. All these petty objections are simply expressions of the prejudices and bigotry that exist right here in this room."

"That'll be quite enough, Dean" said the President, now bristling.

"Mr. President, I call for the question," I hollered. "And I would like a division of the house—so stated in the minutes as to indicate who voted for the class and who voted against it—so that everyone in this college and in this community can find out who voted for what."

"That won't be necessary. We never do that," he replied. "Look, the hour is getting late, and we're probably all tired . . . saying things we don't really mean. I suggest we have the vote at this time."

Ethnic Studies 37, Marimba band, one unit, four hours,

passed by one vote. The President counted hands out loud to make sure everybody understood. Ralph's Dean, the head of the science division voted for the motion. Bless his pointed head. I hadn't figured him for that, but since one of his instructors was involved, maybe something changed his mind—trickle down loyalty maybe. Nevertheless, his vote made the difference. But then, of course, three no's were over there at Henry's probably drinking margueritas and peering down the waitresses' blouses. The Lord works in mysterious ways.

*

On my way over to drop off the mountain of handouts I had collected, I thought about what my evaluation would probably be like this year. It's not as though I hadn't been told to cool it in the past. "You might well re-evaluate your inclination to take overly assertive positions inasmuch as they at times risk becoming counter-productive," my immediate boss had written

As I passed the music building, I heard the muffled glow of the marimba from inside. Good Lord, are they still at it? I couldn't resist dropping in to tell them the good news. Everybody cheered.

After leaving the room, outside in the hall, I met Mrs. Fernandez's son Philip, here to collect his younger sister.

"Hey, Dean, you know what happened? The Migra (Chicano slang for US Immigration and Naturalization Service) just shot a guy this afternoon up in Vineyard City. An illegal . . . just a kid . . . 16 years old. They told him to stop, but he got scared and ran. So then one of the cops plugged him . . . POW . . . just like that. He's in the hospital. Nobody seems to know if he's gonna make it."

"Philip, I'm sorry . . . "

"And you know what? I'm telling Lydia to screw this stupid Marimba band. They're just a lot a' fuckin' coconuts—brown on the outside and white on the inside—and Ralph is the biggest one of all. Fawning and begging and dancing to that stupid Mexican hat dance so that a bunch of society ladies can say, 'Oh, isn't that just so fuckin' cute—absolutely adorable!' . . . But then it always ends up with us eating shit, doesn't it, Dean—or gettin' shot!" He pulled open the classroom door, hurried in, and slammed it after him.

I was stunned. Just walked down the hall staring at the floor. I looked at the stack of papers I was lugging. On top was that cover sheet—wrinkled, Scotch-taped, and spit-smeared. Instead of re-doing it, I ought to just leave it exactly as it is, frame it, and hang it on the President's door for everyone to see: a Declaration of Dependence—Summa Scum Laude—a monument to shame, disgust and hypocrisy.

"Workin' kinda late, ain'tcha, Dean." It was Curly, the janitor. He sidled up to me, stopped, leaned on his broom and talked in hushed tones, sort of confidential, the words oozing out of the side of his mouth. "Jesus Christ, Dean, you hear that damned noise from those Mexicans over there? They've been goin' on like that all afternoon. I don't see how you guys allow that . . . Look, you're a smart guy. Tell me something? What's wrong with American music? In English?—If they don't like our music or our ways, nobody's stoppin' 'em from heading back. Hey, I don't see any of 'em swimmin' south over the Rio Grande—only north." And that's when he pushed himself off his broom and sauntered back slowly to where he had left off, and commenced sweeping.

*

"If Music Be The Food Of Love, Play On"
"Twelfth Night" by Wm. Shakespeare

memorabilia

The minute I walked into my parents' house that afternoon, I knew something was wrong. Mother was scowling and got right into my face.

"That man! Your father!" she shouted. "That man! Er macht mish ganz verrückt! Crazy, he'll drive me yet !" Her brown eyes, now much magnified by the thick glasses they gave her after her recent cataract operations, glowed with anxiety.

"All week long he's been sawing away on that cello . . . You don't understand. He thinks he's Arturo Toscanini or some big-shot musician . . . Hour after hour—day after day! Never leaves it alone . . . And now today, every twenty minutes, he runs out to the car to see if it will start . . . Listen, he got all dressed up hours and hours ago . . . And doesn't even have to be there til seven o 'clock. The man thinks he's maybe twenty years old . . . And here he is going on eighty . . . I tell you that father of yours is pushing me over the edge. Ganz verrückt ist er! Always with this crazy music of his—symphony this and orchestra that! And stubborn! Well, I don't have to tell you. You know! Like one of those mules back there on the ranch!"

And that's exactly when he popped in out of the bathroom—right on cue like in a soap opera. Totally lost in a loose-fitting tuxedo, he'd been in there unsuccessfully trying to tie his bow tie. And raised himself up to his full height—all five feet, two inches—and faced me.

"There, now you see what I have to put up with!"

Then wheeled around to confront his wife of over fifty years. "I have to check the car to see if it'll start, don't I?"

One look at his face and I realized we were in deep trouble. He couldn't go looking like that. As usual, he'd nicked himself in lots of places—some of them still oozing. And on top of that he missed a lot of scruffy white hair under his chin and under both ears—Right away I knew what the trouble was—that stupid used razor blade sharpener he'd purchased a couple of years ago. Good gravy! It's not as though he didn't have enough money to buy a few razor blades. No, it's just that he wants to prove the junk he buys from all of his crazy catalogs is just the greatest. You see, my father is a gadget junkie—a big-time sucker for any and all manner of crack-pot inventions, contraptions and thingamajigs—like the pen you always see in his shirt pocket, the one that's supposed to write in four different colors but hardly ever writes in even one—just leaks colored ink all over his shirts—or the two little lights that you pin onto the frame of your glasses so you can read in bed—as they blind you in the process. But the item that infuriates me the most is that utterly useless used razor blade sharpener. It's only about twelve inches long with a scrawny little metal handle that goes back and forth over a thin honing belt. You put your used razor blade in at one end, push and pull for about five minutes and then according to the manufacturer, out pops "a brand new surgically sharp razor blade." Baloney! The truth is what comes out is duller than what went in.

But he'll never admit it! Like all the rest of the garbage he buys, he's convinced those blades are "just wonderful!" So that every time the man shaves, his poor face ends up looking like a bloody battlefield. Mother is right; he can be infuriatingly stubborn about a lot of things—especially about all those idiotic thingamabobs.

*

Well, I dragged him back into the bathroom and straightened out his face. That took about ten minutes. Then tied his bow tie while he constantly kept looking at his dollar watch at the end of a cheap chain insisting that he had to leave right away because they were going to be taking pictures of the orchestra before the concert tonight. That was the reason for the tuxedo and the bow tie.

So he grabbed a clean white handkerchief out of their bedroom, stuffed it into the breast pocket of his jacket, gathered up some sheet music from his music stand and rushed out to the car, a

1934 Plymouth coupe with a rumble seat in the back, into which he had already loaded the cello. The time was about five o'clock.

He climbed in nervously, slammed the door, started the motor, waved us good-bye, but let the clutch so fast that it killed the motor. Then for a couple of minutes the car wouldn't start at all—probably because it was flooded or because it was mad at him. He punched the starter so many times that I was afraid he would run down the battery. But it finally did kick over, and he floored it till it screamed—at which point, he put it in gear with a loud grinding sound, let out the clutch so fast that it shot forward like a race horse. That got him to take his foot off the gas and onto the brake, and the thing almost stalled again. But after a lot of starting and stopping, lurching and stalling, hiccupping and coughing, thank God, the little Plymouth finally stuttered down the driveway.

He was so short that he always looked under the steering wheel to see where he was going. When making a turn, he never rotated the steering wheel in a continuous arc, but only moved it a few inches with one hand while holding the wheel steady with the other, then frantically repeated the same motion over and over until he completed the turn. Mother and I watched anxiously as he executed a wide turn on to Arthur Avenue just fast enough to cause the cello in the rumble seat to lose its center of gravity and careen from one side of the seat to the other with a loud bang. Ouch! That hurt! Luckily he carried it in a strong wooden case.

But they were finally off, Jacob Hugo, his cello and his music, off to Roosevelt High School here in town to perform with the newly formed Fresno Philharmonic Orchestra under the leadership of Haig Yakjian, its original conductor.

*

About an hour later I drove Mother over to the school.

*

I must have been around four or five when I first heard classical music, and it came from right inside of our own apartment back in the old country, Germany, way before the advent of radio or television. Two live men on violins, another on the viola, and my own father on the cello playing chamber music right there in the middle of our own living room. Real people creating wonderful live music! It filled our apartment with amazing sounds, harmonies and rhythms. The music was exciting, animated and reverberated through every room, even out front and into the back yard. "When I grow up," I thought, "I'd love to be a part of that."

They usually played on Sunday afternoons, but on this one Sunday, about half-way through the Haydn, the Fricks who lived right above us in our apartment building hung out a large Nazi flag from their front window which was right above ours. Not on a flag pole, but from two strings tied to either end of their window sill so that the thing dangled right next to the outside of the building. Then lowered it from both sides so much that it completely covered our whole front window. The sun shining through it left our living room an eerie crimson.

As soon as Father realized what was going on, he slammed his cello down on the floor. Furious, he bolted around the room pointing his bow up at the ceiling. "It's Frick! Frick, upstairs!—It's because we're Jewish. He doesn't want you men to play music with a Jew! And here I am a decorated war veteran—nearly lost my life fighting for the Kaiser!" he shouted. "An he's never even been in! Just runs around town in his shit-colored uniform."

"Shhh, Jacob," one of the men put his finger in front of his lips. "Not so loud. They'll hear you."

"Look, we've never done anything to that man," Mother cut in. "Nothing! Never!" she exclaimed. "So how can one live like this? What can one do? Where can one go?"

Of course, Frick's message wasn't only for us. It was for the others as well—telling them that in the Third Reich, Christians do not play chamber music with Jews—which they never did again. And soon Jacob, along with several other Jewish musicians, was dropped from the local musical scene—the symphony orchestra, chamber music societies—everything. The year was 1934.

A few months later, it all came to a head for him when, just by coincidence, he came across his long-time buddy, Theo. The two of them had known each other for at least fifteen years, ever since they served in the army together. And so now, how could Jacob not notice the large swastika sewed to the front of Theo's jacket?.

"So, Theo, I see you've taken to wearing a swastika on your jacket, eh?" he asked.

"Oh, it's down at work, Jacob. You know, they insist I join the party," Theo replied. "Look, if I don't join and go along with all this," he pointed to his jacket, "I'm sure I'll lose my job."

"And I suppose soon you'll be putting on a brown shirt and pants and running through the streets with the rest of these hoodlums?"

"Hey, look, a man has to do what a man has to do to survive, right? Surely you understand that, Jacob?"

"I only understand one thing a man has to do," Father scorned, "and that is to act like a decent human being."

The argument grew louder and more heated; one word led to another; until in the end Theo thundered, "Damn it, Jacob, get this through your thick head because I'm only going to tell you once—Adolf Hitler is more important to Germany than Martin Luther!"

That did it! That was the limit! And that very night the two of them, Father and Mother agreed that, as far as our family was concerned, there was no hope left in Germany. We had to get the hell out of there! They considered many possibilities—France, Portugal, Holland, England, Palestine, Spain—but decided on America. Yes, they would try to get to America—he 55, she 45. And so, the following week he got on a train to Stuttgart and applied for visas for the four of us at the American Consulate. He was able to get a temporary visitor's visa for himself so he could establish a "beach head" for us, and left for New York.

Month after month, Mother and brother Fritz and I waited for some word from the consulate, but nothing. And as each day passed, our environment became more hostile and intimidating. First, we children brought home notes from school announcing that Jewish children were no longer allowed in public schools. In the meantime, just about all the stores in town posted signs in their windows "Jews Not Allowed," and throughout the city, on almost every corner, you saw large hate posters with images of fat, piggish-looking men with prominent hook noses and piercing eyes wearing skull caps with large captions at the bottom "Juden Raus!" "Jews Out!"

Finally, in May of 1935, a little over a year since we had applied, we received our visas and immediately started packing, gathering up two centuries of roots into all that was allowed for the three of us, one steamer trunk and two suitcases. Off we went by rail to Cherbourg in France. Once there, we boarded a tiny ferry out to the huge four smoke-stacked Cunard White Star Liner, SS Aquitania anchored in deep water. They extended a narrow gangplank so that we and a few others could climb aboard, and I can still remember us struggling to carry our heavy suitcases and father's priceless Czechoslovakian cello on board.

After the war, we learned that just about one-third of German Jews like us were able to escape; the other two-thirds remained trapped. The world witnessed their desperate decline— their social isolation, economic ruin, the destruction of their property, personal injury and unbelievable humiliation. And in 1942, the "Endlosung der Judenfrage," ("The solution to the Jewish Question") commonly known as "The final solution." became a reality. The remaining Jews were crammed into box cars and sent to concentration camps where they were either starved, shot, or gassed to death!

*

It was great to see Father again, and in Brooklyn, we settled into a third floor walk-up in a crowded tenement. He barely scraped by by selling California wines to some of his erstwhile European customers. Still, without fail, several evenings a week, he tuned up the old Czech and sawed away—Dvorak, Mozart, Haydn, Beethoven—and always ended up with his tour de force, a well known war horse from the old days—Luigi Boccherini's cello concerto in B flat. Though only moderately tuneful, it featured monumental jumps and leaps, prodigious fingering, fierce scales and acrobatic cadenzas. Like so many cellists, he worked his jaw back and forth as he charged ahead, bowing furiously.

You'd suppose most neighbors might well object to that kind of treatment, but since the lady of the house in the apartment next door, a recent immigrant from Scotland, still harbored grand ambitions of becoming an opera star, we were treated to nighty scales from her as well just about every night. So that in effect, the two musical geniuses of the third floor in that tenement on Fourth Avenue in Brooklyn canceled each other out, while the rest of us just smiled, shook our heads, and wondered if maybe we too should become musicians.

*

Since New York was still in the crush of its greatest depression and since he was relying on making a living from only the commissions on his sales, he jumped at the chance of getting a full-time bookkeeper's job on a huge ranch owned by the California wine company whose products he had been trying to sell overseas—all for the promise of $80.00 a month and a free house for his family to live in.

Which meant that once again we carefully gathered up our belongings, packed them into the same steamer trunk and suitcases which had accompanied us across the Atlantic, and watched them, along with the cello disappear into the belly of a rumbling Greyhound that took three and a half days to bring us all the way across America to the rural town of Madera in the heart of the grape and raisin country of Central California.

*

The ranch was huge and contained several thousand acres of grapes. In every direction, as far as you could see, there were Thompson seedless that dried into sweet, sticky raisins as well as deep red Zinfandels and Muscats that the winery processed into sweet dessert wines. And on many of those balmy evenings, after a real scorcher of a summer's day, with all the windows wide open hoping for a merciful north breeze, you could hear the farm hands strumming their guitars and singing prideful, spirited Mexican harmonies on the porch of the bunkhouse—paso dobles, valzas, huapangos.

But if you listened carefully . . . that's right—Boccherini! Jacob Hugo found that by sitting on a couple of large, upside down packing crates they called "sweat boxes," normally used to store raisins, he could amplify the sound of his cello, envelop and totally lose himself in the music he loved so much.

And that's the way it went for many years until the owner of the ranch, the man who had originally hired him in New York, died, and the ranch came under new ownership, and everybody was let go. Luckily the two of them were able to piece together the tiny reparations they received from West Germany with their Social Security and with some help from us kids, managed to move into Fresno and squeeze by.

*

Father sat in the very last row of the cello section of the orchestra, and from where we were sitting, he was mostly hidden from view. But though we couldn't see him, I knew he was there. I could feel his spirit—the cockeyed optimist who tried to forget all that had happened to him and his family but still believed you can sharpen dull razor blades. All you have to do is tune up your instrument, practice a little and let yourself go, involve yourself in the mystery of music, and give birth to those magic tones and rhythms that prove our lives are still worth living.

"If music be the food of love, play on!'

*

The last piece the orchestra played that night was Tchaikovsky's Sixth Symphony, "The Pathetique," a wrenching work from the mind of a guilt-ridden, tortured genius. "While composing it," read the program, "he would often burst out into tears."

There was so much applause after they finished, the conductor asked them all to stand and take a bow. Hey, what do you know? There he was. Now you could see him, the little bald-headed guy holding his cello and smiling, and Mother leaned over my shoulder. "He did it pretty good tonight, the old man," she said. "He's a little dotty, you know, but he's all I got . . . And after all, he did get us out of that Schweinerie—that pig sty!"

*

When he got to be in his late eighties, he lost the upper body strength to tune his cello properly. Couldn't turn and push the pegs in hard enough to make them stick. So, without telling a single soul, he traded the wonderful Czech for a real cheapo which used metal tuning gears like you see on guitars. We all knew he got snookered a ton on that deal, but just like with all his other goofy gadgets, he insisted that his new cello played "Just wonderful!"

"Can't you hear it?" he would ask you as he played away. "Doesn't it have a beautiful tone?"

*

No matter. Jacob Hugo died at 96.

*

And if there is a heaven for musicians, surely he's up there now sitting on some overturned sweatboxes sawing away at the Boccherini with a dollar watch hanging from his music stand so he should know exactly how long he'd been practicing.

And you know what? Every once in a while, the maestro himself comes over and puts a hand on his shoulder. "Come on now, Jake," he tells him. "pick up the tempo a little, eh." And looks him straight in the face, "And another thing, when you gonna get a decent shave?"

*

Chris

fiction

With an audible click, the minute hand of the big school clock up on the wall of the boardroom jumped from 24 to 25 after one. The note had said "One o'clock sharp." That's when the hearing was supposed to have begun. All the principals except the Chancellor and the school board members were present and accounted for. But since the board wasn't there yet—now almost a half hour late—nothing could begin.

It was one of those awkward moments in life just before mortal combat when the air hangs still and heavy. Outside, the weather was leaden, overcast and threatening, but in here it was hot and stuffy. Everyone was apprehensive and preoccupied, weighing the possibilities, wondering how things were going to turn out this afternoon.

Conceding the metaphor, we sat in overstuffed chairs on opposite sides of the long polished oak table in the center of the room directly below the dais. Chris, whose job was on the line today, sat exactly across from me staring into space. His wife Moira was on one side of him; his union rep on the other. The two lawyers from the County Counsel's office were on our side of the table alongside our college President. To their right was my immediate boss, the Dean of Instruction, and to his right Sid Snyder, the Personnel Director; and then there was me—I'm Chris's Dean. Over in the corner on neutral ground, an attractive young woman court reporter, specially hired for the occasion, waited patiently behind her small transcribing machine on a tripod, doing her nails.

"Wonder how much she gets an hour," I asked Snyder softly.

"Plenty," he frowned, "and we're payin' for it."

"Which is all the more reason for the board to get their lazy asses in here and get this thing started," said the Dean of Instruction. "Believe me, I've got better things to do."

Looking at Chris I realized that for the first time in the three years I've known him, he was actually spruced up. Wonder of wonders, his wavy red beard was neatly trimmed, his hair combed and braided in a neat little curl in the back, and he was actually wearing a shirt and tie, regular slacks, a sports coat, and real shoes.

Finally! The side door flew open and all six of them burst in. The five board members hustled up to the dais and scooted in behind their name plates followed by the Chancellor, who seated himself in the middle of the group and clicked on his microphone. "It's my fault," he said nervously. "It took so long to get waited on at that restaurant. Sorry about that."

We all stood up and saluted the flag, and then, the Chancellor asked for the hearing to begin.

That, of course, was the lawyers' job. They had already spread three long parallel columns of documents out in front of them, each one halfway on top of the other—performance evaluations, personnel files, minutes of meetings, parental and student complaints, memos, directives, policy statements, excerpts from the education code. I know the process. One by one, they'll place these into evidence and conclude that in the aggregate there was enough incompetence; insubordination and bad judgment to warrant giving this guy the ax.

"Good afternoon, ladies and gentlemen," he started out. "My name is Cliff Houseman, and this is my colleague Beverly Glass. We both work in the County Counsel's office which is charged with representing the college district in this matter . . ."

He was friendly enough—short and rotund, dark and balding, with bushy black eyebrows that appeared to be growing out of the tops of his horned rimmed glasses. "The immediate charge here," he went on, "is that Mr. Christopher Mallory, who we believe is present," he nodded at Chris, "while employed as an art instructor with the district did knowingly allow the consumption of a quantity of alcoholic beverage—namely six 12-oz. cans of beer—to take place while he was in charge of a college art class on May 26, 1970. Actually the class in question was being held at Mr. Mallory's home during the time normally reserved for the final examination . . . Now the consumption of alcohol by anyone, especially students, during class time is clearly prohibited in the Education Code in the strongest terms. In addition, according to our investigation, the alcohol charge appears to be only the tip of the iceberg, the culmination of a long history of anti-administration attitudes and acts, of general intransigence, of blatant and dangerous violations of campus policies, and of grossly uncooperative and unprofessional conduct. It is for these reasons that the administration recommends that Mr. Mallory be terminated at this time."

He looked up at the Board. "As you know, ladies and gentlemen, before such a dismissal can be consummated, the law stipulates that there must be a hearing in front of the governing board . . . That's you folks, of course," he smiled, "and that's, of course, why we're all here this afternoon."

As he labored on, I studied Chris's expression. Though attentive and sober, he didn't appear particularly concerned or contrite. His face mirrored the points the lawyers raised. Sometimes he smirked, even chuckled to himself quietly, but mostly his expression was the one I've become so familiar with—a gentle defiance, puzzlement, a distant preoccupation.

At times, Moira acted surprised at what she heard. She's evidently had no idea of the extent of her husband's problems here at the college. Occasionally, she wiped her eyes with a small lace handkerchief. Somehow, the pain of all this seemed to add to her natural and stunning beauty. Wispy blond curls framed her classic features and immaculate complexion. It's a mystery to me how a woman like that could remain loyal to a flake like Chris after what he put her through all these years. She must really adore the guy.

*

Back in 1968—I was still teaching English—that's when they hired Chris. Vietnam was already boiling—lots of student demonstrations against the war—administrators plenty nervous. At the time, the gossip was that Chris got his contract over half a dozen other applicants because he appeared to be the least "far out" of those who had applied. "Art is a touchy area," the President had warned, "and we sure as hell don't want any long-haired, tree huggin', peace-nick types on board." So that the hiring committee was relieved to find Chris—the only candidate with a decent hair cut—dressed in a suit and tie, his shoes polished. And most convincing of all, the guy was a graduate of a university in Utah. Nobody ever heard of a troublemaker coming from Utah. Sure, teaching ability, artistic talent, communication skills, experience and all that were considerations, but at the time, safety was paramount. And that's why they hired clean-cut, super-safe, Utah-raised Chris over all those other applicants. But now, three years later, the worm had turned 180 degrees in the opposite direction—constantly gnawing, tunneling, and boring into those he considers to be "the establishment."

To my way of thinking, the first step in Chris's epiphany came when he volunteered to teach an art class at the veterans' hospital just north of town. Once a week he got on to the oversized elevator up to the crafts room next to the 'long-term' ward up on the sixth floor. And that's where he met them—the gray men back from Nam—mostly in wheelchairs or leaning on walkers—uncoordinated assemblages of mind and body—stumps for arms and legs—concave hollows over metal plates in skulls and faces where bullets had entered or exited—their movements slow and spastic—their conversation jerky and confused—smoking constantly.

In just a couple of years his revulsion of America's role in Southeast Asia converted him into an outspoken opponent of the war. Nowadays, you could always find him right up there in front at anti-war rallies and demonstrations. Long ago, he exchanged his suit and tie for a linen toga that set off a crude iron peace symbol strung from a rustic chain around his neck. He quit wearing shoes altogether—just bare feet in sandals. Both hair and beard grew into a scruffy red tangle. A new persona had emerged—a flower-child—a strange form of non-rebel rebel—a vassal in the "hippie" kingdom. Over time, there was talk about drugs and alcohol. I investigated all that the best I could, but couldn't find anything.

Meanwhile, his classes had become sanctuaries for all

levels of Vietnam protesters—those not yet drafted—those thinking of fleeing the country to avoid being taken in, and those returning home from the war. It was standing procedure in the counseling department that whenever they were confronted with a debilitated veteran, one fighting dementia, obsessed with demons and screaming in the night, they quickly enrolled him in one or more of Chris's art classes.

He dropped everything to join them at their functions. He made himself available at all times—days, nights, weekends, vacations. They had become his top priority. He carried signs and clapped, shouted, chanted, sang, and prayed as he marched along with them. He anguished and feared for them when they burned their draft cards; he sat in sweaty courtrooms at their trials and kept vigil outside their jail cells. More than once Moira came to see me and asked me to talk to him, to intervene. "He respects you," she told me in that sweet voice of hers. "Maybe you can get him to ease up," she pleaded. "So that the fire won't consume and burn him up altogether . . . You know, Dean, he brings these guys home—tries to clean 'em up at our house . . . tries to sober and dry 'em out. That's not his job, Dean," she anguished, by now in tears. "It's all so scary."

At the same time, I constantly received a steady and adamant stream of complaints about Chris's 'non-teaching' from just about all of our traditional students, often accompanied by notes and letters from irate parents. They told me that Chris's classes were just a big joke. There was no discipline at all—no regular assignments—no teaching going on whatsoever. Students were simply allowed to walk in and out at will while Chris ranted and railed about the war.

And one time, I got this frantic call from Mrs. Clarksdale, our home economics instructor. "Dean," she twanged, "did you know that one of your teachers, ole' Friar Tuck I call him, whom I've had the distinct misfortune of havin' to teach right next to for the past couple of years, is havin' another one of his 'happenin's' today? I mean, I know the guy's loony tunes, but at least, up to now he's been sorta quiet and left us alone . . . But now—like today—all of a sudden, he's drivin' us up the wall . . . Dean, you gotta get over here and see what's goin' on. I mean this is gettin' totally out of control!"

And the minute I got there, I realized that she was absolutely right. My God, the sounds coming out of that room were unearthly, weird, like something left over from the stone age. There was a large sign on the door—hurriedly scrawled in big red letters on a long sheet of white wrapping paper—"DO NOT ENTER! Big things are **HAPPENING** IN HERE! KEEP OUT! This means YOU!"

I tried the door, but it was locked. Judas priest! That's dynamite! Strictly illegal. What if there were a fire or an earthquake or an explosion of some kind and the firemen or paramedics couldn't get in! Or students out! Luckily I spied a janitor who opened the door for me . . . Bedlam! Lunacy! Total chaos! About ten students were grouped around a long cardboard tube— the type you find in the center of a roll of carpeting. At each end, about half of them were roaring into it as loud as they could— nothing that made any sense—just wild screams and incoherent babble. Other students were beating on the tube with sticks and their hands. Some were painting it with large brushes and poster paint. The place reeked of incense which was smoldering in several coffee cans on one of the work tables. Still others were singing, groaning, and grunting. Over in the corner a girl was pounding away on what appeared to be a children's drum set. And Chris, oblivious to it all, sat on the other side of the room totally preoccupied as he looked out the window and strummed his guitar.

The blood ran to the top of my head; I could hear my pulse clicking away in my ears. "Mr. Mallory," I shouted, "Mr. Mallory, please stop these people!—MR. MALLORY! MR. MALLORY!" I heard myself actually yelling, "Please get these students to stop this madness!" But he just sat there. "MR. MALLORY!" I repeated even louder as he finally looked up and registered surprise to see me and smiled. "CHRIS! CHRIS! I implore you, please get these people to stop this madness—PLEASE!"

He looked confused, but did as I asked, but they didn't hear him. So he walked over to the tube and asked each student individually.

When the students finally, finally calmed down, he introduced me. "And this, class, is his honor, our new Dean," he smirked forcing a nervous laugh.

But me, I was still in panic. "Look here, people," I shouted. "I'm sorry, but we can't have this. This racket has got to stop—and it's going to stop—and I mean RIGHT NOW!—It's going to stop!"

Whereupon, from over in the corner, the girl who had been beating on the drums imitated a trumpet fanfare, "Tat-ta-ta-rat-tata. Sieg Heil, mein Führer!" she taunted giving me a Nazi salute. "Mein Führer hatt geschpoken," she crowed and hit the drums even louder than before, and the students roared with laughter.

"I THOUGHT I TOLD YOU TO STOP THAT!" I screamed at her livid. "And you will stop! Do you hear me?"

I then turned to the class, "Look here, people—where do you think you are? This is a college, not a mental ward. This racket you've been making in here is disturbing every room in this whole damned building. We've had complaint after complaint here from other teachers. Surely you understand that the students who take classes next door or down the hall have just as much right to an education as you do. Is that so hard to understand?"

After another minute or two of fuming and railing, I sensed they were beginning to calm down and listen. Thank God! Somehow I was finally beginning to reach them.

"Now I'm directing all of you to conduct this class in such a manner so as not to disturb any of your neighbors around here. Is that understood?" Silence. As I started to walk out, I remembered about the door. "And another thing, Mr. Mallory, this door is NEVER, EVER to be locked while students are in here. Is that understood? What if there were an emergency and those who came to help you in here couldn't get in?"

Later on that same day, Chris came over to the office as I had requested, and I asked him, "Chris, what in the name of hell was all that about this morning?"

"Oh, just a 'happenin', coach," he shrugged. "Lets the students get their feeling out. You know, about the war." He acted nonchalant, as though the total madness over there that morning amounted to absolutely nothing. "They have 'em all over," he said. "You know, at the universities . . . everywhere, even in high schools," he laughed.

"Well, now, Chris, please relieve me of my anxiety. Please assure me that we're never, ever gonna have anything like that again. I don't care what you call them, what they're about, or who does them. I'm simply not going to tolerate that kind of disruption ever again. Tell me I'm right, Chris?"

Like at so many other meetings, Chris remained disarmingly courteous and pleasant. He listened carefully, appeared cooperative, never argued. "Sure," he answered, "Sure, Dean. I know where you're comin' from." That's his favorite expression. "I know you've got a job to do."

Still I got the feeling that his acquiescence will probably be short-lived, done only to please me, to be nice. His heart isn't in it. I can feel the resistance. Sooner or later that inner flame of his will re-kindle and there will be more rebellion. Not that he's against me personally. I actually believe he likes me, but I have to face the fact that as an employee here at the college, Chris Mallory is a first class screw-up . . . Oh, well, at least he's agreed not to have any more 'happenings' for the time being . . . At least I think he realizes that his classes have no business disturbing their neighbors . . . So maybe things will improve.

*

But I tell you this war is going badly. Every night, the TV is full of it. More riots in schools and colleges and minority communities all over the nation—more strikes and sit-ins, more marches and demonstrations.

The police and the National Guard are out in force. You see them beating people with batons, mowing them down with water cannons, sicking police dogs on them, dragging limp bodies into vans. The President and the governors and the senators and the generals and the mayors and the chiefs of police and the college presidents are all screaming 'law and order.' Overseas, unending lines of refugees carrying punishing loads on their backs and heads, babies squalling, stream from one unpronounceable place to another. And from Hanoi, deeply disturbing interrogations of American POW's by their North Vietnamese captors. And then, from thousands of feet up, the TV cameras track rafts of bombs floating down in graceful symmetry onto the verdant jungle below. They explode in concentric patterns lifting rosettes of fire, smoke, and debris up off the screen. And soon we hear the rat-a-ta-ta-tat of an unexpected jungle firefight. Helicopters drone in to pick up the wounded and the dead, while back home surly soldiers gurney their fallen comrades down long ramps from cavernous jets and stack their dead comrades, now enclosed in black plastic body bags, in neat rows on the tarmac. And finally the President comes on and tells us he needs more troops.

*

Winter turns to spring, and as the days grow longer, Chris decided to hold his classes outside. That way, he won't be bothering anybody. One evening he asked his students to bring balloons. They pumped them up so they would fly; then the young people painstakingly decorated them. Each balloon had the name of a young man from the college who had gone to war, been killed or wounded painted on it. Photos, if available, were taped on. The idea was to release the balloons and never retrieve them. Just let them drift away. It was a way of experiencing death Chris explained—Just let their souls float into the night. A way of letting go of someone into whom you've poured time, effort and conviction—someone you have imbued with your spirit and essence—someone to whom you have given love and passion.

They waited for sunset, formed a small circle on the practice football field next to the stadium, sang hymns to the accompaniment of Chris's guitar and just about when everything was almost totally dark, he gave the signal, and all the balloons were launched.

Swaying and rotating, they slowly rose in the evening breeze and floated lazily up and over the high diving board at the edge of the college's pool; then flew higher and higher, over the football field and past the campus radio tower with its pulsating red light, still turning, twisting, swaying, and dancing in the breeze. On occasion, one of the taped-on glossy photographs glistened with a flash of light as it reflected the setting sun. But shortly, the images and the balloons themselves faded into the night, and all that remained were the students' fragile voices in the dusk.

"Amazing grace! How sweet the sound!"

*

About a week later, every one of my bosses sent me a memo ordering me to shut down the launchings. First was the Chancellor, "We've gotten a number of complaints from angry homeowners and taxpayers about these balloons, ostensibly launched by a faculty member in your division," he wrote. "They are landing in their neighborhood. Besides being a nuisance to clean up, they tell us the balloons are filled with anti-war and anti-government propaganda. If this is true, it grossly jeopardizes our friendly relations with our community in general as well as our taxpayers. SO I'M URGENTLY REQUESTING THAT YOU LOOK INTO THIS MATTER AND STOP THIS ILLEGAL ACTIVITY IMMEDIATELY."

Next, came the President: "Is this all we can teach our students—to learn how to send up trouble-making comments and pictures? Why in the world didn't you stop this instructor from pulling off a crazy stunt like this?"

And finally, my immediate boss, the Dean of Instruction wrote: "This is really embarrassing—The Chancellor actually told me on the phone that if these damned balloons don't stop, they might even jeopardize flights going in and out of our airport! So get your hippie friend to quit sending up his condoms immediately—ASAP—like yesterday! THIS IS IMPORTANT! What's he smoking anyway?"

After reading all that, I dropped everything and headed up to Chris' room. But when I got there, he already knew why I came. "I know where you're comin' from, Dean" he assured me. "Don't worry. The launchings have stopped."

*

So he moved his classes back indoors, and with only six

weeks left in the semester, announced that his students would be putting on an art exhibit. Since the college had no art gallery, it was to be mounted in the hallway outside his room.

The idea of an art exhibit put on by a guy with a history like his sparked immediate controversy. Some said there wouldn't be any art out there at all, just anti-war propaganda, probably a lot of frontal nudity, shock porn, and explicit sex. Then the President's cabinet called for a strict policy on art displays—that is, what can and what cannot be shown on campus. The student council said that was 'prior restraint' of artistic expression and free speech and amounted to censorship, a Constitutional issue. The faculty senate held for the cabinet, but the teachers' union supported the students. Daily, our mailboxes were bombarded with polemics from one side or the other—editorials, demands, proposals, white papers, manifestos.

But in the end, the President had the hammer. The opening sentence of his administrative directive concerning "The Display of Artistic Artifacts on Campus" set the tone: "While the College does not wish to suppress new ideas, opinions, or efforts at creativity," he opined, "and while we are ever mindful of the First Amendment to the United States Constitution, and while the College is philosophically opposed to the prior restraint of the selection of artistic material to be displayed in public, one needs also to be mindful of COMMON SENSE and COMMON DECENCY." What all that meant is that he would only allow those paintings, sculptures, and art objects to be displayed which had been pre-approved by a committee of his choosing.

A week went by as we waited for him to appoint the review committee—to see who was on it. But Chris couldn't wait. So one night after everyone had left the building, he and his students put up their exhibit. They hung exactly twenty paintings with nylon fishing line from a molding high up on the walls so that the paintings wouldn't damage the plaster in any way. And when the college came to school the next morning, there it was. *Fait accompli.* The exhibit was up!

And when I walked into my office that morning, there were

already six phone calls waiting for me to call back—including two from the President. The shit had hit the fan! I returned his calls, but he wasn't available. Fearing the worst, I hurried over to take a look. Thank God, nothing really hard core! Most of what was up there seemed innocuous enough, even silly—rushed and amateurish. I certainly wouldn't hang any of those dumb things in my house, but then what do I know? I was sure a couple of pieces would raise hackles. One was of a seated girl wearing shorts with a bull's eye target painted right in her crotch. Another of a swan with an inordinately long beak, an imperious scowl, and long extended wings which framed two sagging breasts. The swan faced Mrs. Clarksdale's room, and it was impossible not to make the connection. Later, I heard she spent the whole morning in just about every administrator's office protesting vehemently.

And when we finally connected, the President was beside himself. "I've been over there to see your mess!" he said enunciating every word carefully. "Tell me something?" he carried on, "How is it possible for this exhibit to be up there at all?—contrary to my explicit instructions?—Nothing! Nothing was supposed to be on display until the committee had approved! It has to come down immediately! Right now! Is that clear?"

"Yes, sir—Sure—Of course."

"And I think it is high time that you have a serious talk with this instructor and advise him that his continual flaunting of campus rules and regulations will have the most serious consequences . . . As a matter of fact, I think that you yourself need to consider how best to control these loose cannons in your division. Frankly, I'm just a bit tired of coming to school every morning and being confronted with yet another crisis . . . This isn't the first time, you know. It's a question of control. Who the hell runs this school anyway? And please understand this, if you can't keep your people in line, well, maybe it's time we brought someone on board who can."

So I rushed over to the art exhibit for the second time. A camera crew from our local TV station and a newspaper reporter from the *Evening Record* were already ambling through the hallways, filming, interviewing, taking notes and photos. But then, Chris had already made his next move. All the paintings had been turned to the wall—only blank canvasses showed. And in the bottom right hand corner of each frame there was a simple 3 x 5 card with the inscription "ART AT PHILISTINE COLLEGE 1971."

"Chris, the President is in orbit," I told him. "He just chewed my ass out but good . . . So I guess I'm more than a little upset. Look, you deliberately disobeyed his specific orders. What can I tell you? All this is going down into your permanent file . . . And the paintings have got to come down immediately! Do you understand? By God, if you don't take 'em down, and right now, I'll pull 'em down myself!"

"Sure, sure," he answered. "I understand," he repeated. "I know where you're comin' from," he said with that stupid grin on his face. "Don't mind me—Do what you hafta'," he told me. "Don't worry, Dean. We'll take everything down," he said as he ambled away looking ecstatic —and that burned my ass.

"Blank Art Stirs Protest," was the headline in the evening paper.

*

At the end of the semester, Chris invited all his classes to his house for their finals. In one class the students collected some money for refreshments and came back with two bags of chips, a six pack of soda and another of beer. One of the girls in the class told Mrs. Clarksdale all about it, and she in turn called every member of the Board of Trustees and every administrator whose name she could find in the directory.

Chris admitted to the beer. "Liquor is serious," I told him and wrote up a formal report which I shipped up the line with the recommendation that he be suspended for one semester without pay.

Thinking they had an open and shut case this time, the three of them—the President, the Director of Personnel, and the Dean of Instruction—believed they had enough to fire the guy outright. And so, without consulting me, they called in the lawyers.

*

After the attorneys finished, Chris's union rep pleaded for him. All the charges except the beer were bogus, he told the board. The college has no business telling a qualified instructor how to manage his classes. "You're infringing on this instructor's academic rights," he said looking at Chris. "As far as that goes, you can't fire people just because you don't happen to like their attitude or their politics . . . So what are you really sacking this guy for? A six pack of beer? Please! What a joke! I think we just all happen to know that there are plenty of instances where this college knows of students drinking a little beer at a college function—and often a lot more than a 'little' beer—like for example at sports events and rallies and banquets—like for example at dances and carnivals. And never, never, ladies and gentlemen, has that ever resulted in an instructor's dismissal. Let's face it, it's just that the administration here," he pointed at all of us sitting on our side of the table, "has got it in for Chris Mallory. He's a burr under their saddle because he's against the war in Vietnam—and that's the long and the short of it, isn't it?"

And before he sat down, he introduced a nun who had been waiting in the back of the room, though I don't remember seeing her come in.

"I've been in one of Mr. Mallory's art classes all semester," she told them in her Irish accent. "A healin' spirit he is, ladies and gentlemen, in such troubled times."

And then Moira got up. "Chris hasn't been himself for several years," she told them sobbing openly, wiping her eyes. "He knows he did wrong . . . And he's willing to change . . . He told me he would." She put her hand on his shoulder. "Give him a chance—please!" she pleaded. "He's not a bad person or anything like that."

And then it was my turn. "There's no getting around Chris's infractions," I told them. "But no matter how this thing turns out, we all need to remember that Mr. Mallory here has performed a service to our returning veterans. Everybody agrees about that."

And finally, the Chancellor asked Chris himself if he had

anything to add.

He stood up slowly, smiled, and shook his head. "I'm sorry I've inconvenienced all of you," he said. "I can't believe that it took two lawyers more than a whole hour to recount all my sins," he laughed nervously. "Man, that's a long time . . . Like I said, I apologize for having put you all through this. I mean, I'm sure you have better things to do—like sell things and make some money. But whatever you decide, believe me, I don't blame you. All I know to say is that I'm sorry for what happened . . . and what I'm most sorry about is that we're in this dreadful Vietnam War . . . But then firing me isn't going to change that, is it? . . . I'm sorry, folks, but it's not gonna stop this crazy war," he said staring up at the ceiling. For a few seconds he looked like he was going to talk some more, but decided otherwise and sat down.

*

In just a week, they announced their decision: "One year's suspension without pay with confirmation of the completion of an approved counseling program before being reinstated." The ruling was considered a setback for the administration.

*

And so this fall, Chris is gone. Some of the students miss him, and in a strange way I miss him too—some of the time at least. Along about Christmas, I got this cardboard tube—the type large calendars come in. It was from Chris. Inside, there was a letter and an anti-war poster he had painted. He now lives in the Mojave Desert having run away from the four-week counseling program he had enrolled in. "I met up with a couple of ancient prospectors out here in the desert," he writes, "and I'm keeping house, or rather cabin, for them while they're off on long trips trying to find precious stones out there in the desert. I play my guitar a lot and paint posters. The one I'm enclosing is for you, Dean. Hope you like it. Merry Christmas. Chris."

"P.S. Moira filed for divorce. She is a good woman, Dean. I pray she will go with God. Peace, and please tell the lawyers I quit."

*

Become a 'Late Bloomer' Like it Says in the Brochure

fiction

Paul dashed across the parking lot as fast as he could and bounded up the stairs two at a time because he simply had to get to English before the bell rang. Purcell was tough on you if you came late, and Paul knew that with his problem, he couldn't afford that. The only other time he'd been late, he hadn't even bothered to go in and just ate one of the three absences Purcell allowed you.

They had asked him to stay late at the hospital that morning to help set up the oxygen for a new patient who had pneumonia, and the time had slipped away. Out of breath and panting, he finally made it to the top of the second floor landing, and quickly glanced at his wristwatch. Four minutes to go—thank God! He would make it.

Taking roll in Purcell's English class didn't take all that long because here at midterm, of the 32 who originally started the class, fewer than half were left. Those who remained appeared lost in the room since he made them sit in their original seats. Purcell himself had kicked two out for talking, one for refusing to take off his baseball cap, and one for cheating. The rest dropped themselves.

In his late 50's, pudgy and graying, with a penetrating gaze through curved tinted glasses, Purcell's quiet, deliberate way of speaking belied his reputation among the students. "It doesn't look good, people," he told them in that special, slow, clipped cadence as he handed back the first draft of their research papers. "At this rate, I don't know what I have to do to get you students to follow simple instructions."

And when Paul saw the large F emblazoned on his paper, he felt a surge of anger. Those same pages that he had worked on so diligently all weekend were now bleeding with red ink from Purcell's stupid marks and comments. He had thought the absolute worst he could possibly get was a C. The F was numbing.

Paul poured over the pages. All in all, there were five

grammar errors—two "agreements" and three "run-on's," and six "sp's" for spelling. He quickly got out his dictionary and looked up each of the misspelled words. And what infuriated him was that only two of the six were actually misspelled. It was just that Purcell had told them that if their compositions weren't typed, they would have to be written in cursive writing—no printing. And whenever all the lines inside a word weren't connected properly, it would be counted as a spelling error. Paul had four of those.

But he wasn't the only one who was upset. Stephanie, who sat in the middle of the first row took her paper, crumpled it up with a flash of disgust, muttered something under her breath, and angrily hurled it at the wastepaper basket in the front of the room. She missed.

"Is there a problem, Miss Piper?" Purcell asked slowly.

"Yes, Mr. Purcell, there is a problem," she imitated his slow intonation, seething.

Purcell looked away, waited a moment and smiled politely. "Would you like to tell the class, Miss Piper, what you seem to be so upset about?" There was a pause. "Or is it that you've decided to be a troublemaker bent on disruptin' this class?"

"I'm not disrupting a damned thing," she answered, her voice breaking. She stood up and hurriedly walked over to where the paper had landed, picked it up and straightened it out. "Look here, Purcell, this is a damned good paper. I know it's a good paper," she said holding it up. "I worked real hard on it, and for you to mark me down because the loops 'above the line,'" she mimicked, "aren't as long as those 'below the line' is unfair as all hell! Other English teachers don't put you through this kind of shit! Now . . . you wanted to know what my problem was. Well, that's it in a nut shell!"

"Miss Piper, you may not know this, so I'm going to tell you now—I don't allow vulgar or obscene language in my classroom. So you may just leave—right now. You're dropped, Miss Piper. You're through. Just collect your things and leave."

"Oh, you think you're kicking me out, don't you? Oh, no— that's not it . . . not it at all, Purcell. Because I quit . . . Quit—like just about everybody else in here. Look around the room, Purcell—hardly anybody left. They're all gone, aren't they, Purcell?" she yanked her books out quite deliberately from the small book shelf underneath her desk and slammed them, one by one, into her blue backpack.

"Well, we're waitin', Miss Piper."

"Hey, maybe you were born in a hurry, Purcell, but I came out slow and easy." Her comment provoked a slight titter as she walked over to the door swinging her arms and hips loosely in an exaggerated manner, opened it, walked through, and slammed it shut.

Never raising his voice, Purcell mused. "It's just a case of followin' instructions, people. If you're goin' out into the business or professional world, or if you students are plannin' on pursuin' your college education at a four-year institution, they'll expect you to be able to follow instructions, to be able to write so that it can be read properly. This is <u>college</u> English, people. You're not in high school any more."

And that's when Paul raised his hand.

"Yes, Mr. Stacey."

"But . . . I . . . I . . . I . . . d . . . d . . . d . . . don . . . se . . . se . . . see the . . . that a wo . . . wo . . . word shoul . . . be ma . . . ma . . . marked w . . . w . . . wrong . . ."

His head was swinging from side to side, turning, twisting, struggling—his face flushed and strained, tongue protruding between lips as he inhaled with a great slurp, and snapped the rubber band on is wrist. "If the . . . the . . . the lines . . . lines . . . lines . . ."

Purcell interrupted. "Mr. Stacey," he said kindly, "we really don't have time to wait for you to complete your question right now. Perhaps you can try again later when you're more composed."

For the rest of the period Paul was in crisis. It was another instance of frustration, failure and defeat that had dogged all his days since he had arrived on this earth some 36 years ago—all centered around his inability to get the words out. He now hardly heard anything that was going on in class though he was aware that Purcell seemed to be lecturing about footnotes.

He had put off taking his English till this semester—which he thought would be his last. The realization now that without English he wouldn't be able to graduate was paralyzing.

The paper he had turned in was about his major—"Inhalation Therapy." Now that he was apprenticing at the hospital three mornings a week, he felt he knew enough about the subject—why people needed a supplement of oxygen, ways to use oxygen at home and in the hospital, and how the treatment benefited patients.

What he couldn't understand is how Purcell could get by with all these stupid rules. The paper had to be 20 lb. bond with at least 15 percent rag content. It had to be folded lengthwise with your name, date, class, and assignment title on top—all within meticulously strict margins. The ink had to be black; he wouldn't accept blue—not even blue black. Even the paper clip had to be of a certain kind and had to be centered exactly a half inch from the left margin. On and on—so petty and unfair. He pulled the rubber band taut on his wrist and let it go with a snap.

*

Paul grew up way out in the country on a dairy. After he finished high school, he worked with his father out there on the farm until the old man came down with emphysema and sold the place. They invested their money and moved to town. Paul remembered his father gasping for breath and how he had learned to attach all those hoses to the green tank, assemble and open the pressure valves, adjust the regulator, and make sure the safety equipment was in good condition. He recollected how the oxygen had given his dad strength and relief before he passed away. "Inhalation Therapy" they called it. Well, he thought, if he could help his own father, he could help others—people in hospitals and rest homes. He could study at the local junior college—get a certificate, a degree, a diploma, a job—become a "late bloomer" like it said in the brochure. But then Purcell had noted in large red letters, "The subject of this research paper is somewhat too broad. It will have to be narrowed down before it meets my criteria for acceptability."

He contemplated going to see him in his office. Purcell always told them they could do that. Maybe he could ask him if there was any chance at all of passing the class? Maybe he could ask him how to narrow down the paper so he would accept it? No . . . no, he would just block again as he always did and embarrass himself. It wasn't as though he couldn't fix the mechanical errors—He could—connect all the stupid lines inside words. But to narrow down the subject would surely mean having to practically start from scratch again without any assurance that Purcell would actually accept his paper, and by that time the deadline for dropping classes without penalty would probably have passed, and he would be stuck with an F. Purcell seemed so unreasonable. Maybe the best thing to do would be to drop the class altogether and try again later with another teacher—but then he wouldn't be able to graduate.

And what would he tell his mother? He knew exactly what she would say. "Paul, Paul, I'll be sixty-seven years old this September . . . Not going to be around much longer . . . If you don't graduate, all this inhalation stuff that you worked on so hard all these years will just go for nothing, just wasted . . . Paul, Paul, I'm so nervous and worried from all this." And like always she would find some reasons to blame him for the mess he was in like because he was drinking too much coffee, or not eating right, or not taking his vitamins, or not going to the single's club at church so he could meet a girl—because if he did all that and met a girl, he wouldn't stutter any more.

Women. How could he ever even think of having anything to do with women? With his speech problem such a thing was impossible. And yet his memory took him back to the day so many years ago in his junior year in high school when that beautiful Italian girl with the long dark hair, the olive skin, and the thick accent who lived on a vineyard farm not far from their dairy got on the school bus one morning and sat right next to him.

"I'm ah soph-o-mor-eh. What ah you?" she asked. But he couldn't answer. "You hous-ah on ah dairy, no?" she asked. "Got ah lotta cow, eh? And de big bull too, no?" she laughed. By this time he had pulled out a blank page from his binder and had written "I'm not rude. I just don't talk good. Sorry," and gave it to her. After she read it, she smiled and said "Oh," but never sat next to him again.

Nor was it that he didn't know about male and female. Because all through those long years with his father out on the dairy, he regularly witnessed the bulls mount the cows to "freshen" them as his dad would tell him. He watched their glazed eyes and dull expression as they humped with morose efficiency, and every spring pulled wet calves from their mothers' wombs—who, upon seeing the world for the first time, bleated in great terror amid the bloody, gelatinous muck of their arrival. It was a melancholy business, sex.

And once, while he and his parents were vacationing over in Santa Cruz, he drifted into an adult bookstore where he purchased his first copy of *The Mermaid's Joy Book,* the one with a topless, beckoning mermaid on the cover, the one he slid under the mat in the trunk of their Cadillac. And from that first acquisition he amassed a small collection which he carefully hid in his room, ordering under an assumed name from the mermaid's bawdy catalog. After every order, he made sure he was the first one out to the mailbox each morning so he could intercept his prizes— "intimate, torrid, uncensored, X-rated." And year in and year out he succumbed to repeated cycles of desire, resistance, arousal, capitulation, regret, shame, and depression, pouring over the well-worn copies of the mermaid's lustful images as well as his remembrances of that exquisite Italian girl who was so attractive and had once sat so close to him on that school bus.

As for his speech defect, well, from infancy there had been a succession of speech teachers, clinics, and therapists. They searched his throat with funny instruments and looked down with tiny flashlights and mirrors. They felt his neck, chest and abdomen—had him inhale and exhale. Had him make sounds— hum, sing, talk. Had him divide words into syllables—vowels and consonants. Showed him on the charts where to put his tongue, lips, and jaw. Had him sound out words—and repeat and repeat and repeat. Had him memorize the charts, and drill, and drill, and drill. The last one, who called herself a "language acquisition specialist," even put a rubber band on his wrist. That way he could pop himself and be distracted whenever he felt like he was going to block—At least that was the theory.

Purcell was still droning on about footnotes, the words falling slowly and evenly like the persistent beat of a clock that refuses to run down. He had passed out several sheets having to do with the subject. "Remember, people," he insisted, "*ibid., loc. cit.,* and *op. cit.* are abbreviations. They need to have periods after them, and since they all come from Latin words, they need to be italicized. That means, if you're writing in long hand, you underline them. And you can't just use one line to underline two words. That will be considered a spelling error."

Paul looked around the room. Most of the students sat there in a daze—stupefied and groggy. He folded his arms in front of him, laid them on the desk and let his head and shoulders fall gently.

"Sit, up, Mr. Stacey," Purcell admonished.

Paul raised up, glaring.

"I don't believe in convertin' my classroom into a dormitory. If you don't think you can last out the period without goin' to sleep, perhaps you ought not to come at all."

Mercifully, the bell rang, but they still had to wait till he said it was all right to go.

"I expect your footnotes to be ready next time, people. And please try to get them right." The students started closing their books and folding binders in anticipation of leaving, but he wouldn't dismiss them until there was total silence.

Still scowling, Paul walked around the back of the room so he wouldn't have to face Purcell close up and ducked out.

When he got out into the hall, he was surprised to see just about everybody from the class bunched together in a lively knot, talking excitedly.

"Paul, Paul, come here," said one, "We're gonna go see the

Dean. Wanna go?"

He walked over hesitantly.

Stephanie, the girl who had been kicked out, was in the middle of the group.

"The first thing I did," she said, "was call my dad at the bank, and he told me not to take any more shit from that guy and go straight to see the Dean. I know I shouldn't have cussed him out, but then he shouldn't have flunked my paper. All I did was show the Dean my paper—and when he saw all that stuff about the loops above and below the line, he just shook his head and asked me if the other students felt the way I did. And I told him hell yes. So he wants us all to come see him."

"Right on," said one.

"You bet. Let's go." said another.

Paul listened intently. Sure, he'd be glad to see the Dean. No, it was more than that; he wanted to see the Dean so he could show him his paper too—not only marked down, but failed, because all the stupid lines weren't connected.

"But if we go and see the Dean," admonished a heavy set girl, "and Purcell finds out, we'll all be in big trouble."

"B . . . B . . . But . . ." Paul was trying to say something.

"Look, you guys. I have to make it through this class," interrupted another girl. "Otherwise, I won't be able to go to the university next year, and my folks will like, kill me. I'm sorry, guys, but I can't take a chance."

Paul stiffened. They just couldn't miss this opportunity. For a split second, a single shining moment, he saw everything quite clearly. It was like a shaft of light had landed on him. All of a sudden everything that had been so fearful and dark and complicated jumped into focus with an almost audible click—bright, hard-edged, and clear. There it was for all to see—this man Purcell was a petty tyrant who wasn't going to terrorize Paul Stacey any more—not even for a second.

No! They just couldn't miss the opportunity to see the Dean.

So he stepped forward right into the middle of the group.

"Stephanie is r . . . r . . . right," he said. "We don't have to take this stuff no more. Look, if every single one of us goes, and threa . . . threatens . . . to drop his class, and we all really d . . . d . . . do it—I mean for real. DROP IT, then there wouldn't be anybody for him to teach. Not a soul! The room would be empty!" he laughed.

A strange silence came over them . . . They looked at each other in amazement realizing that for the first time in their memory Paul had actually spoken. He had actually talked! Even he couldn't believe it because he turned around sheepishly as if he was trying to find out if there was anybody behind him who had said all that.

"Paul, Paul, you talked!—You talked!" said Stephanie. "Unbelievable!"

And they all started shouting at him, shaking his hands and patting him on the shoulders.

"You did it, Paul. You actually talked!"

"A way to go, Paul."

"Hey, man, great job!"

"Give me five."

"You did what you been wantin' to do all semester. You actually talked. Good for you!"

"All right, all right. So, let's get this show on the road," Stephanie reminded them. "Let's get our fannies over there to that Dean's office . . . and bring your papers . . . Come on." She put her arm around Paul who by now had a big grin on his face, as they headed over to the Dean's office.

*

Franz Weinschenk was born into a Jewish family in Germany in 1925. He and his family were lucky to escape from there in 1935. After graduating from Fresno State University in California, he served in the Army for two years and then became an instructor and Dean at Fresno Ctty College where he worked for 60 years. He currently lives in Fresno with his wife Sally. An enthusiastic runner, biker, and swimmer, he recently was the first over 90-year-old to finish the Merced Gateway Triathlon. He served as the host of a public radio show called "Valley Writers Read" featuring local writers for over twenty-five years.